MW00412614

ON THE
PROWL

A BAD THINGS NOVEL

New York Times and *USA Today* Bestselling Author

CYNTHIA
EDEN

This book is a work of fiction. Any similarities to real people, places, or events are not intentional and are purely the result of coincidence. The characters, places, and events in this story are fictional.

Published by Cynthia Eden.

Copyright ©2016 by Cynthia Eden

All rights reserved.

Cover art and design by: Sweet 'N Spicy Designs

Proof-reading by: J. R. T. Editing

Build 2

PROLOGUE

"There are...things you don't know about me," Julian Craig said gruffly, his faint British accent slipping into his voice. "Things I didn't know how to tell you."

Rose Kinley forced herself to smile. "Whatever it is, I'm sure it's not as bad as you're making it seem." And he *was* making it seem bad. Her heart thudded in her chest as she stared at him. They were in the Florida Keys, a virtual paradise, and the moment should have been perfect. Julian had taken her to a private home on the gleaming water, and they were standing on the balcony as the waves crashed below them. She'd been dating Julian for nearly two months — two of the best months of her life.

Rose was pretty sure that she was falling in love with him.

Julian. Tall. Dark. Handsome and so very sexy with his powerful build and those mysterious, golden eyes. When he came into a room, she couldn't look away from him. She'd actually felt pulled toward him from the very first moment that they met.

"Rose, do you believe in monsters?"

A surprised and nervous laugh escaped her. "Monsters?" She put her hand on his chest and felt the strength beneath her touch. "You mean the boogeyman?" She smiled, teasing.

He shook his head and Julian didn't smile.

The moments ticked by. *Is he serious?* Her own smile vanished. "No, I don't believe in monsters. I'm not a child to be scared of the dark." She stared up at him. "I know there is evil in the world." This was so *not* the conversation she'd anticipated when he brought her to such a romantic setting. *So much for those plans.* "Robbers, killers...I know they're out there. I see stories about them on the news every night."

"I'm not talking about bad humans." For a moment, she could have sworn that his eyes gleamed. Sometimes, they seemed to do that...to be brighter. To almost glow. A trick of the light or the dark or *something,* she was sure. No way were his eyes actually glowing. "I'm talking about real monsters," he continued gruffly. "And, love, you need to believe in them because they are out there."

Her heart lurched in her chest. *No, Julian, please, don't be insane. You were so wonderfully perfect.* "Are they?" Rose asked him carefully. Her friends had warned her, but had she listened? Oh, no. *If a guy seems too good to be true...*

"Yes, they are out there. They hide in plain sight and humans just don't see them."

If he seems too good to be true, then he probably isn't all that good in the first place.

She swallowed and her hand fell away from his chest. Rose pulled in a deep breath and despite the heat of the night, it seemed to chill her lungs. "Do you...see any monsters right now?" Probably something she should know.

He growled. Goosebumps rose on her arms because it was such a deep, animalistic sound. That was one of the things about Julian. He had sort of an animal attraction vibe going on. A wildness that he barely held in check. Maybe that wildness was what had first drawn her to him. She'd taken one look at Julian and thought...

He isn't like other men.

Now she knew why...it was because the guy might just be certifiably insane. Monsters walking around with humans? Sounded like he'd definitely taken a break from the meds.

"I'm dead serious, Rose. Fuck, I knew you wouldn't believe me. I have to show you..."

She backed up a step. "I-I thought we were just going to have a nice night out. You don't need to show me *anything* about monsters—"

His left hand lifted. A strong, powerful hand. One tanned by the sun with long fingers and…and claws that were sprouting from the tips of those fingers.

Claws. *Claws.*

Rose shook her head. That wasn't possible. She squeezed her eyes shut for a moment, but when they opened again, the claws were still there — and growing longer with each moment that passed. Long and wicked sharp claws.

"I'm one of the monsters, love."

Her head whipped up. She stared into his eyes and they were *definitely* glowing. That wasn't normal. *Glowing eyes. Claws from his fingertips. Oh, my God.* Even his face shape had altered a bit, becoming sharper, harder.

She took another stumbling step back. "This isn't funny. I don't know how you're doing this, but stop the joke."

"It's no joke." His voice had changed, too. Gone deeper. His words were more growl than anything else. He lifted his right hand, and it was changing, too. More claws. Long and dark and sharper than a knife.

Rose shook her head — over and over — and then she did what any smart woman would do when her lover suddenly sprouted claws. She turned and she ran.

"Rose!"

She didn't slow down, she just ran faster. She flew through that house and rushed down the stairs that would take her to the ground floor. She didn't hear him behind her and that scared her because she was sure he was trailing her. She grabbed for the door and yanked it open—

Only to have it immediately slammed closed again, by Julian. He hadn't just trailed her, he'd caught her, all without making a sound.

Her breath heaved out and she whirled to find another way out. But...she was trapped. He'd trapped her between his hard body and the wood of the door. His eyes were still doing that scary glow thing and she was too afraid to look down and see if he still sported claws. "I-I want to leave." She tried to sound calm. Rose was sure she failed.

"Let me explain..."

Explain claws? "You already did. You're a..." *Monster.* Rose couldn't get that word out.

"I should have stayed the hell away from you." His gaze swept over her face. "But there was something about you, from the first moment. I saw you, and I wanted you more than I've ever wanted any other woman."

Her heart was about to jump right out of her chest. He wasn't touching her, but she could feel his heat surrounding her. He was so big, well over six feet, and he dwarfed her own five-foot-five frame.

His dark head leaned toward her. "But I *never* wanted you to fear me."

"Then maybe you shouldn't have flashed your claws," she blurted. Because how was she not supposed to fear those things? They were like knives that had just grown straight from his fingers.

"I'm a shifter. It's what I've been since birth." Dark stubble lined his jaw. "If I could change who I was, I would. Trust me, I've wished to be different more times than I could count but I never wanted it more..." He swallowed. "Never more than when I met you."

A shifter. That meant...he turned into some kind of animal or something, right? "What do you...become?" Was she seriously having this conversation?

"A panther."

Right. Sure. Because of course he wouldn't turn into something cuddly and sweet. He *would* be a panther. Raw power and danger and claws that could rip her throat open in one swipe.

She felt dizzy. Rose really didn't want to faint on him. "I need you to let me leave."

"That's the last thing I want to do." And then he was locking his hands around her shoulders. She couldn't help it, Rose flinched, but his claws didn't slice into her. He touched her with the hands and strength of a man, not some kind of beast. "You think I've *ever* told another human what I am? That's against the rules. I'm not

supposed to tell mortals, but you're different."
His gaze still blazed. "Because you're mine."

When he touched her, her body reacted. It
was like a heat burned between them, one that
raged and destroyed everything in its path,
everything but the white-hot need and passion
that erupted. He touched her, and she wanted. It
was a desire unlike anything she'd ever felt
before. And, yes, maybe she had thought it was
unnatural at first…

Then she hadn't cared.

But now… "What did you do to me?" Rose
whispered. "How did you make me want you so
much?" Even then, when she was terrified of
him, she wanted him. Her breasts were aching,
her body readying when she should be running
as fast and as far from him as she could.

"I think you were made for me."

Rose shook her head.

"And I was made for you."

She didn't believe in soul mates. She hardly
believed in love. She —

"I will *never* hurt you," Julian vowed.
"Believe that, if you believe nothing else. I told
you the truth because I don't want to lie to you. I
want you to know all of me. Everything. No
secrets and no —"

But he broke off, his eyes widening in alarm.
Bam! Bam! Bam!

She heard the thunder, as if from a distance. She heard the blasts and she felt the wooden door shake behind her.

Then the pain came, erupting through her body. Her right side. Her left. Her back and then — then straight through her chest.

Julian was shouting and jerking her away from the door. She grabbed his arms, holding tightly, and she looked back over her shoulder.

There were…holes in the door. As if someone had…shot through the door?

She could feel a warm wetness on her body. Julian had her in his arms and he was running through the house. He rushed up the stairs and put her on the bed.

"Don't move, love. Just…fuck, stay here, I'll take care of them. I'll take care of *you*."

Rose tried to speak, but couldn't. A faint moan was the only sound to escape her lips. She tried to lift herself up, but…something was wrong. She couldn't move her legs. And the pain that had wracked her just moments before?

She didn't feel it any longer.

She didn't feel anything.

But she could hear screams. Desperate, terrified screams that seemed to shake the night itself. And she heard the inhuman snarls of a beast.

Her breath whispered out and her eyelids sagged closed.

She was dying, and Rose knew it. Someone had shot through the door. The bullets had torn into her and now...now her life was over.

***

"I hope you know what you've done."

That voice — low and oddly sinister — pulled Rose from the darkness. Her eyelids flew open and she sucked in a greedy gulp of air.

"Be sure you hold up your end of the bargain, panther." Again, it was that sinister voice talking. One that seemed to reek of power and danger. "Because there is a price for the gift I've given."

Her gaze shot to the man speaking. He was tall, with dark hair, glinting eyes, and a face that seemed to be cut straight from stone. For just an instant, she actually wondered if she was looking into the face of the devil. But then he smiled at her...

Rose didn't wonder any longer. She *knew*.

"Welcome back," he said.

Back? Her gaze jumped to the left and she saw Julian...Julian — who was wearing only a pair of faded jeans and who was *covered* in blood. The coppery scent reached out to her and Rose found herself licking her lips.

I like the way it smells.

What in the hell? She jerked upright in the bed, a bed that was also stained with blood. Her blood. Her hands flew over her body, searching for the wounds that had been there before, but now they were gone. No torn skin. No bullet holes. No pain at all.

"Wh-what happened?" Rose whispered. Her throat seemed parched so she swallowed a few times and licked her lips. "I was...hurt."

"But you're not any longer," the mysterious man said. "Amazing, isn't it? The price some people will pay to keep the things they value."

She wasn't a thing and she didn't think she liked that mystery guy. "Who are you?"

He shrugged. He wore a suit, a perfectly pressed suit that seemed so out of place in that room full of blood. "Call me Luke. All my friends — and my enemies — do." He stalked toward Julian and clapped a hand on the other man's shoulder. "See? She's as good as new. Well, with a few minor adjustments, of course."

She slid from the bed and stood on trembling legs, feeling at a terrible disadvantage. "What's going on?" Rose struggled to remember. "I was...shot."

"At least three times," Luke offered helpfully, even smiling as he shared that tidbit with her. "Or was it four? One bullet severed your spine. Rather nasty."

She looked down at her legs. Rose remembered that she hadn't been able to feel them. A tear slid down her cheek. *I feel them now.*

"And what weak assholes shoot through a door, anyway?" Luke demanded to know. Her gaze flew back to him as he shook his head in disgust as he released Julian's shoulder and turned the force of his rather creepy stare onto her. "Using heat sensors, trying to take out Julian. Not caring who got in their way. Hardly the sporting thing to do." His smile hardened. "I sure hope they're enjoying hell."

Severed your spine...And what weak assholes shoot through a door, anyway? His words echoed in her ears. She stumbled away from him and found herself backing into the nearby corner as her shoulders hit the wall. If some bullet had severed her spine, she wouldn't be standing right then. She wouldn't even be moving at all.

Terrified, her gaze darted around and she realized that every piece of furniture in that bedroom—every piece but the bed she'd been in—had been wrecked. The dresser was smashed to bits. The chair had been clawed open. The *walls* were even smashed—deep holes and gouge marks were in them. *What is happening?*

"A thank you isn't out of the question," Luke announced as he released Julian's shoulder. He waited a beat, as if he expected someone to suddenly shout out thanks. When no gratitude

came, he sighed. "I pretty much bent the laws of
nature for you, lady. So...yeah, you're welcome."

"I'm having a nightmare." There. That made
sense. Julian wasn't a monster. He hadn't grown
claws. She hadn't been shot. Creepy Luke wasn't
there. This was all —

"You *are* the nightmare now, sweetheart."
Luke gave her a chilling smile. "And again,
you're welcome."

Her gaze snapped toward Julian. Why hadn't
he spoken yet? And why was he staring at her
with that twisted expression of grief and relief on
his handsome face? "Julian?"

A muscle flexed along the hard line of his
jaw. "I wasn't going to let you die."

Her stomach was twisting.

"Technically, she *did* die," Luke supplied
helpfully as he tapped his chin. A big, ominous-
looking ring curled around his finger. "And I
brought her back. Undead style."

She grabbed at her shirt once more. Her
blood-covered shirt. There were holes in her shirt.
Bullet holes? *OhmyGod, yes, they are.* But no
wounds were on her body.

"So, you'll need to know a few things." Now
Luke seemed brisk. "Sunlight won't kill you. That
old story is total bullshit. My asshole brother
started circulating it centuries ago. Leo is such a
bastard."

"Julian?" She whispered once more. "What's happening?"

His gaze seemed tormented. She *felt* tormented.

"You still breathe. Your heart still beats," Luke continued. "I mean, if it didn't, your body would start to decompose. Your flesh would rot. You'd be all gross and disgusting and basically a zombie. Which you are *not*," he added hastily when Julian glared at him. "But since you still have a heartbeat and brain function and what not...that does mean you *can* die. See, that's where the stories always go wrong again. Once more, courtesy of my dick brother."

She didn't care about his brother and Luke was just talking nonsense.

Why was Julian not speaking?

"So you can be killed with the usual methods," Luke's voice was flat. He snapped his fingers. "Pay attention here, okay? Focus. This shit is important."

Rose blinked.

"A gunshot to the heart, drowning, stabbing...you get the idea." His hand did a little roll in the air. "You'll die, but you'll come back. Lucky you."

"This isn't real," she mumbled. It *couldn't* be real. Her stomach wasn't just twisting any longer. It was knotting. Cramping.

"You'll come back," Luke nodded, "but you'll be damn thirsty. Just remember that blood is always of paramount importance for you. Drink up, drink, drink, drink."

He'd just told her to drink blood.

And…

Her teeth were burning. Stretching?

"There they are." Luke clapped his hands, as if proud. "Right on cue." His head cocked. "Gorgeous fangs, by the way. They'll help you with that whole blood drinking issue. You can also compel humans, to a certain extent, so they'll pretty much just offer their throats to you." He sighed. "A word of warning, though, try not to kill your prey. That will just attract my brother's attention and, as previously noted, he can truly be a pain in the ass."

Her fingers were over her mouth and she touched — fangs. Honest-to-God fangs were coming out of her mouth. Her canines had extended to wicked sharp points and when she talked — "This isn't happening!"

When she spoke, she actually had a little lisp.

Luke just laughed. "You'll get used to them. Give it time."

She wasn't giving this *anything*.

"Now, I said you'd come back from death, but there are a few exceptions." Luke turned his back on her as he paced around the room. "Don't ever take a stake to the heart. Your heart is *key*, my dead. *Key.* And don't get yourself burned to ash. Oh, and if you lose your head — "

She ran for the bedroom door, but Julian suddenly stepped into her path. He'd moved fast. Way, way too fast. He didn't touch her. His hands were clenched at his sides. "I'm...sorry. I couldn't let you go."

Her breath heaved in and out of her lungs. Her teeth burned in her mouth and hunger was clawing through her. "What did you do?" Talking was hard with those stupid fangs in her mouth.

"I made a deal with the devil."

Someone tapped her shoulder. "That would be me, sweetheart."

She didn't look back. She couldn't take her eyes off Julian. "I don't believe in the devil."

"Maybe you should," Luke said, sounding annoyed now. "Maybe it's time for you to start believing in a whole lot of things."

She had to get out of there. Rose shoved against Julian and he actually backed away. She flew through the doorway and ran — ran faster than she'd ever gone before. In seconds, she was out of the house and barreling down the street. Her surroundings seemed to pass her in a blur and then —

Julian's hands curled around her. He stopped her. Just appeared right in front of her and caught her hands in his. "I won't always be able to catch up to you," he muttered. "Luke just gave me a bonus tonight."

"What is happening to me?" Because that dark, twisting hunger was so much worse and she found herself staring at his neck. She could see the pulse point there. Could almost hear the swoosh of his blood if she tried hard enough.

Everything seemed too bright. Too bright even though it was night time. And she could hear so many sounds...laughter, from people who weren't even on the road. The drumbeat of music from a club that had to be miles away.

"You have to drink because you're still weak." He pulled her closer and even lifted her up against him, moving her so that her mouth was right at his throat. "Go ahead, love, take what you need. I'll always give you what you need."

Her mouth pressed to his skin. Her teeth— she *bit* him and his blood trickled into her mouth. Warm and strangely sweet and soon it wasn't just a trickle because she had to take more. She needed more. She drank and she drank and—

Her hands shoved against him. Julian released her and she stumbled back, almost falling onto the pavement. Her hand went to her mouth and she swiped the back of it over her lips. Then she looked at her hand. His blood was on her skin. His blood was in her mouth.

Julian didn't move. There were two puncture wounds on his neck. Blood dripped down his throat.

You are the nightmare.

"I couldn't let you go," he said again. "I wasn't going to have you die for me."

She shook her head. Horror built in her and she thought she'd vomit, right then and there. *I drank his blood.*

"You're a vampire."

She'd freaking figured that out! "I don't want to be this way." She took another step back from him. "I don't want this!" Drinking blood? Attacking people? "Change me back!"

His head bowed.

"Change me back!" Rose screamed at him. She was a human. She had a great life. She wanted to grow old and have kids and eat chocolate and not be a monster. "Please!" Now her voice was nearly a sob. "Don't do this to me."

"It's already done." He wasn't looking at her.

"You don't get to make that choice." She retreated once more. The scent of his blood was messing with her head. She would *not* bite him again. "It's my life!"

His head whipped up. "It was your death. I came back to that bedroom and you were dying. Did you think I was going to let you go?" He lunged toward her and his hold was too tight as he held her. "I couldn't watch you die. Not you. Not fucking you."

"So you made me into a monster?"

His face hardened. "Rose…"

"Get your hands off me." Fear and fury exploded in her. "Get away from me, *now!*"

Slowly, his hands fell away from her.

"Change me back," she pleaded once more as the bloodlust rose within her. A hunger that made her want to attack.

"I can't." Pain was on his face, but it was nothing compared to the pain that seemed to rip her apart.

"Then stay the hell away from me," she told him and then she was running again. Fast and hard and she didn't look back.

You are the nightmare now.

***

Julian surged forward, but a hard hand clamped down on his shoulder, stopping him.

"I think the woman wants space," Luke Thorne murmured. "So I'd advise you to back the hell off right now."

He didn't want to back off. Rose was in pain. She was terrified. "I have to help her."

Luke laughed. "I think the lady feels you've *helped* enough. I warned you…playing God with someone else's life has consequences."

He knocked Luke's hand aside. "I wasn't going to watch her *die!*"

"Technically, she did die. And I brought her back because I am the all-powerful Lord of the Dark." His words were mocking, but Luke's face was grim. "I broke the rules when I did that. The price paid won't just be yours alone, remember that. She's the first vampire that was created not by birth or by bite. Darkness created her, and darkness will have its due."

His claws were out. "I *need* her." For the first time in his life, Julian had found something — someone — worth fighting for. And fate had tried to take her away from him.

"She doesn't need you. At least, not right now."

"Bullshit. She's scared. She's desperate. She might *hurt* someone."

Luke didn't appear concerned. "Vampires always hurt people. It's what they do. Get it in your head, panther. The woman you knew is long gone. From the minute she sprouted fangs, she became someone else."

His hands were shaking. It felt as if someone had ripped his heart clear from his chest.

"Now, about that deal we made…" Luke's voice was harder.

Luke Thorne…shit, the guy was trouble. Julian knew it. Every dark paranormal who walked the earth feared Luke, and for good reason.

But I had to make a deal with him.

"Let's see if you're really as good of an assassin as the stories say." Luke inclined his head. "I've got some beasts who haven't been following the rules. It's time for them to be stopped."

"Let me just talk to Rose again, I need to —"

The air around them seemed to heat. "A deal is a deal," Luke murmured. "Time to pay the price." Then he laughed. "Besides, it's not as if you won't have time to woo your Rose again. She's a vampire now. She has eternity waiting on her."

She'd vanished from the little road. He still had her scent, though. He could track her. "She didn't even know about monsters."

Luke laughed once more. "She does now…"

CHAPTER ONE

She was evil, straight to her core. A monster to be feared. A creature of incredible power.

She was evil, all the way to her soul. She feared nothing. No one.

So why were her knees shaking? *Dammit.*

Rose Kinley paused just outside of the loud club. The music was making her ears ache and the thick crowd inside had her wanting to turn and run away. She'd never liked crowds. Not in life and not in her *undead* existence, either. But crowds made for the best hunting grounds, and she desperately needed to feed.

So she had to woman-the-hell-up, dig deep to be her new evil self, and go in there and find some prey. Simple enough. Her high heels clicked as she headed toward the bouncer. He was a big, burly guy, a fellow who sported a whole lot of tats and looked as if he feared nothing on the face of the earth.

I want to be like him.

She was down in Key West, a place she did *not* want to be, and her immediate priority was getting enough blood so that she could amp up her power. Once she was operating at full capacity, she'd be fleeing the scene as fast as possible. She had too many enemies in the Keys. Distance was a necessity for her.

The bouncer's gaze swept over her, lingering just a moment on her breasts and her legs. She'd stolen the scrap of an outfit from a nearby shop, knowing it was exactly what she needed to gain entrance to this club. After that brief survey, the bouncer gave a nod. "You're in, lady."

She risked a quick glance over her shoulder, unable to shake the sensation that she was being hunted. Only...no one stared back at her from the shadows.

Her imagination. These days, she always saw monsters.

Rose eased into the club. The music was even louder. A band was on the stage, bouncing around, and the crowd was going wild. The scents of alcohol and sweat were heavy in the air. Couples were making out. The drinks were flowing. And it was feeding time. For her.

Rose found her prey easily. She picked a man on the edge of the crowd, a man who was watching the dancers with a faint smile on his lips. He was handsome — tall, blond, wearing a t-shirt and jeans.

Do this. Don't hesitate.

She walked right up to him and put her hand on his shoulder. His gaze jumped to her face and Rose smiled, hoping she didn't let her fangs show. When she got really hungry, they had a tendency to sharpen without her knowledge. "Are you alone?"

He grinned at her, flashing perfectly even, white teeth. "Not any longer." He gave a low whistle. "I think my night just got way better." His blue eyes gleamed at her.

Poor guy. He had no idea that his night was about to take a serious downturn. She leaned closer to him and let her body brush against his. "How about we go outside?" Rose licked her lips. That was sexy, right? "No one can see us there."

His smile slipped. For a moment, she thought she'd done the wrong thing. Said the wrong words. Maybe she should have tried compelling him instead of using seduction but she was just so weak that she'd been afraid the compulsion wouldn't work.

"You don't have to ask me twice," he replied as he caught her hand with his. In the next instant, he was pulling her through the crowd, heading right for the club's back door. He was stronger than she'd realized at first glance. Muscled shoulders, a firm grip. He shoved the back door open with his left hand and then he turned back to her. "This was so much easier than I—"

Something slammed into him.

Not something. A fist. A powerful hook rammed into the side of her prey's face and he stumbled, ramming into her. She tried to steady him, but the attacker was coming in again.

And, unfortunately, she recognized the attacker.

It was hard to forget the man who'd sent her to hell.

Julian Craig stood there, his golden eyes narrowed to slits as he glared at the man who was now trying to shield Rose with his body. Her prey had turned into her would-be protector, and it seemed sad right then.

I didn't even get his name.

"You're going to let her go," Julian snarled. "Right now."

"Who the fuck are you?" Her prey shouted right back, but his shout didn't carry far. The club was too loud. No one even gave them a second glance.

"I'm the man who is about to kick your ass," Julian snapped back. "Now let her go."

Why was Julian trying to ruin her undead life?

The blond had tensed and she knew he was getting ready to fight. Only it wouldn't be a fair fight because a human would be no match for Julian. It would be a straight-up slaughter, and she didn't have the stomach to watch that, not then.

Her fingers curled over her prey's shoulder. She rose onto his toes and whispered into his ear, "Go back to the music. Go back inside and enjoy your night." He needed to follow her order. Because if he stayed with her, if Julian attacked him full-force, then Rose knew the blond would die.

The guy glanced at her. Already, his jaw was bruising. His gaze was worried, confused. "What?"

"Go back to the music, asshole," Julian blasted. "*Now*."

But the blond shook his head. "You think I'm going to leave you with that psycho?" His stare was on Rose. "Forget it. Let's get out of here together. My ride is waiting out front. We'll get the hell away from this place and him."

A growl broke from Julian. "She isn't leaving with you." His voice hardened even more as he said, "Rose, come to me. *Now*."

What did the shifter want from her? She'd thought to be free of him. Did he just get off on jerking her around?

Rose sighed. As much as she might want to tell Julian to screw off, this wasn't the time. She didn't want to drag a human into her battle with the panther. So she pulled free of the blond and went to Julian's side, frowning all the while. *I'm not happy, Julian. Not happy at all.*

"Good choice," Julian praised, then he slammed the back door shut on the blond's startled face. "Good fucking choice." He locked his fingers around her wrist and hauled her toward the back of the building. "We have to get out of here, now."

She dug in her heels. A quick peek behind her showed that the blond wasn't following. Good for him. "Do you *like* hurting me?"

Julian immediately froze. Then he whirled, stared at her a moment, as if shocked, then he freed her wrist. "I'm sorry, I didn't mean to hold so tight, I—"

She grabbed him and shoved him against the brick wall of the club. "I am starving, Julian. *Starving.*" Because she'd had a truly hellish last few months. She'd been captured by a covert government group who'd lured her in with the promise of *helping* her, only then they'd started playing torture games. She'd been trapped with them until recently…when she'd learned that her asshole of a brother had been the one to set up that twisted group in the first place. She'd just gotten her freedom and she needed to feed. *Badly.*

She did not need to be throat-blocked by Julian.

"You need blood?" He blinked. "You can have mine." He tilted his head, offering his neck to her.

Only there was one big problem with drinking from Julian. He was a shifter — and shifter blood was incredibly powerful. Add that power boost to the animal attraction that she still felt for him — despite everything that had gone wrong between them — and, yes, that equaled a very big problem. Or maybe it equaled a whole lot of big problems.

He's trouble. Bad trouble for me.

"Take my blood," he said, still staring down at her. "Then we have to get the hell out of here because you're not safe."

What?

"Take it," he gritted. He wasn't touching her. She was the one who had her hands slammed onto his chest. "Hurry."

She glanced around. No one else was in the alley. She didn't see anyone in the shadows.

"Do I need to do this myself?"

She felt his muscles shift beneath her hands. She glanced back and saw that he'd lifted his left hand to his throat and his claws were out. Those claws still made her nervous. "Julian, what are you — "

He cut his throat. Not too deep, just a little slice and the blood began to drip down his throat. The smell hit her instantly and her fangs shot out to fill her mouth. She rose onto her toes and licked that little trickle of blood. And at that first taste, the surge of power hit her.

Shifter power. It was like a high, a rush from the best drug in the world. It filled every inch of her body and she just wanted to take and take.

The first time she'd had Julian's blood, she'd been scared out of her mind. The rush had left her shaken and she'd run from him.

She'd been running ever since.

But right then, her hands were tight on him. Her high heels dug into the cement and her teeth sank into him. His hands flew up and locked around her hips and he pulled her even closer to him.

"Missed you..." His gruff whisper. Words that she must have just imagined because there was no way he would ever say that to her. He'd changed her, he'd left her, and he'd nearly destroyed her.

"There she is!" A sharp voice called out, barely penetrating the fog of her blood lust.

"Got to stop, love," Julian told her as he gently pushed her away from his throat. "I'll give you more later. Promise."

She was dazed, still riding that incredible high, but he moved quickly, shoving her behind him just as—

Bam!

Bam!

Those were the terrible noises that still filled her worst dreams. Gunfire. The blasts coming to wreck her life. But this wasn't a nightmare. This was reality. And…*this time,* the bullets didn't hit her.

They sank into Julian's chest. He'd pushed her behind him and the shots had hit him.

"No!" The scream tore from her but Julian…he wasn't falling. He lunged forward and rushed at the two men who'd snuck into the little alley. He slashed out with his claws and raked across the chest of one man, sending him falling to the ground as blood sprayed into the air.

The second man lifted his weapon and fired again, but Julian just laughed. "What is that shit supposed to do? Barely even stings."

The guy stared at his weapon in shock. "It…it knocks out vamps. The tranq is supposed to take vamps down—"

Julian yanked the weapon out of the guy's hand and threw it against the nearest brick wall. The gun shattered. "Your bad luck, mate," he curtly announced. "I'm no vamp." He slammed his head into the other man's. Julian heard the crunch of bones and the shooter went down.

He didn't get up.

Julian looked back at Rose. She'd frozen against the wall. Julian's blood still dripped down his throat. As she stared at him, he raised his hand and held it out to her, beckoning.

He wanted her to go with him? Rose shook her head. "No, thank you."

His face hardened. "I know you don't have a reason to trust me, but I'm not here to hurt you. Your enemies are closing in, love. My job is to keep you safe. Consider me your paranormal protection."

Her gaze drifted down his chest. "They...shot you."

"With vamp tranq. Dumbasses. That was their cock up."

Cock up. Mistake. Right. Sometimes, he used some old British slang. She used to find it cute, charming—

No. Rose slammed the door on their past. That door had to stay shut, if she was supposed to keep her sanity in place.

His hand still reached toward her. "I want this to be your choice. I *need* it to be."

She blinked.

"Come with me. Trust me. Right now."

But she couldn't. After everything that had happened between them, maybe *because* of everything, she couldn't. Sometimes, there was just too much blood and pain and death for trust. "Stay away from me." She kept her back to the wall as she edged toward the mouth of the alley.

"Rose...You *need* me." Frustration cracked in his voice.

Every time they were together, things just ended in pain. Or her death. "Stay away." Then she gave up trying to creep out of his sight. She turned and ran, heading for escape like the desperate woman that she was.

Two vampire hunters had come for her? Who'd sent them? The government? No way would she become Uncle Sam's prisoner again. She wouldn't be anyone's prisoner. And trusting Julian? No, not possible.

Not with the dark truths she'd learned about him.

Julian Craig wasn't some hero. He was as far from a white knight as it was possible to be. He was darkness. *He* was death. He was the monster that she should have feared from the very beginning.

Her high heels clicked as she ran for the parking lot. She didn't hear Julian behind her, but then, he was too good to make a sound. He hunted like the deadly panther that he was.

And his victim never saw him coming, not until it was too late. By then, his claws would be at his prey's throat and there would never be a chance to scream.

Her breath heaved from her lungs and she used her vamp super-speed to get her ass away from that alley. Thanks to Julian's blood, she *could* move that fast again, but the speed wouldn't last without more blood. She needed to hurry and put some serious distance between herself and him.

And…

She knew just how to get that distance because Rose had just spotted a familiar blond figure. Her *intended* prey before Julian had appeared and tried to ruin her night. The blond man from the club was just climbing into the front of his dark SUV. She rushed to the side of the vehicle and grabbed the door before he could close it. "I need a ride." Her voice came out breathless and a little too high-pitched. Hardly the controlled vamp.

The blond blinked at her. "You…wait…what?"

She risked a glance over her shoulder and — shit — Julian was stalking out of the alley. He looked *pissed.* "I need a ride really, really badly." She tried to inject power into her voice as she said, "You're going to give me a ride." The compulsion had better work. She'd gotten that temporary power boost from Julian's blood, so it *should* work but…

The man blinked. "Uh, you want to get in the car?"

"Absolutely!" She took those stumbling words for an invitation and raced to the other side of the vehicle. She hopped in —

"*Rose!*" That deep bellow came from Julian. Oh, hell. He was running for her.

"What's your name?" Rose demanded of the blond as she reached over and took the keys from him. She cranked the SUV.

"Simon. Simon Lorne."

"Wonderful. Great, look, Simon, you need to get us out of here." Julian was almost at the SUV. "*Now*."

He shoved down the gas pedal and they tore out of the parking lot. As they fish-tailed out of there, she heard a long metallic groan, and Rose looked back, frantic, to see that Julian was right behind them. *He scratched the SUV. He was that close – close enough to claw the side of the vehicle.*

"Faster," she urged Simon. "You need to drive one hell of a lot faster." Because she knew the panther would be giving chase.

Simon didn't argue. Maybe her compulsion power was just working extra well. He got them away from the club and they hurtled down the little two-lane highway. Her heart was about to burst from her chest, and Rose kept looking back, terrified that she'd see a panther's golden eyes staring at her.

But he wasn't there.

"You…having some trouble with your boyfriend?"

"He isn't my boyfriend." Okay, so he had been once. *A long time ago.* "He's just a problem from my past." She had quite a few of those. Rose exhaled and forced herself to turn back around and face the front. Slumping in the seat, she said, "Just take the next left. There's a small motel there. You can drop me off and then just forget you ever met me." His world would be much safer once he forgot her.

"Why would I want to forget?" The SUV drove past the road that opened onto the left. "You're the vampire I've been looking for."

It took a moment too long for his words to sink in.

Too long.

Her head whipped toward Simon, but he was already moving. Simon kept one hand on the steering wheel and with his right hand, he drove a syringe into her throat. The needle jabbed into her skin and she felt a hot liquid pour into her.

Dammit.

"You took out my backup in the alley, but I think I can manage to bring you in alone."

"Think again," she gritted out. Then she leapt toward him. Rose drove her elbow into his face and heard the crack of bones. She grabbed for the steering wheel, but he was fighting her. The SUV swerved into the next lane — and Rose heard the loud blare of a horn.

"You're going to get us both killed!" Simon yelled as the SUV flew off the road. It bounced hard and hurtled straight for a tree.

"Lucky for me, I'm already dead." She closed her eyes and waited for the impact.

It was just as hard and brutal as she'd expected. Glass shattered. Metal groaned and she heard Simon screaming.

CHAPTER TWO

Julian Craig jumped off his motorcycle and rushed toward the wreckage. He could smell blood and the acrid odor of gasoline in the air.

"They came right at me!" A woman was yelling. A human who was frantically spinning around in the middle of the street, wringing her hands. "Crossed the line and nearly hit me! Must be drunk or—"

He reached the passenger side of the SUV. Rose was trapped inside, penned by the twisted metal. Broken glass was all around her. Blood trickled from her cheek. "It's okay, love," he said quietly. "I'm here." He grabbed that door and yanked it hard, tearing it right from the vehicle. The metal groaned as it gave way, and he tossed it to the ground.

"Dear God." It was the human female behind him. And she sounded terrified.

She should be.

Julian spared her the briefest glance. "Get the hell out of here."

She took off running.

He bent toward the SUV. The driver was still trapped inside. The blond wanker from the club. His eyes were closed, but he was breathing.

Julian didn't really care about that fellow.

Rose mattered.

He unhooked her seatbelt and carefully pulled her from the car. "I've got you." She was warm in his arms. He could feel the stir of her breath against his neck when he lifted her up, but Rose's green eyes didn't open.

With her held tightly against him, Julian walked away from the vehicle. The scent of gasoline was growing stronger. If that SUV ignited, Rose couldn't be near it. Fire was a surefire way to permanently kill a vampire, and Rose wasn't going to die on his watch — not ever again. That was a vow he meant to take to the grave with him.

"Love?" He eased her down near the road. The woman who'd been screaming before screeched away from the scene in her sedan as her tires left a trail of burnt rubber in their wake. He brushed back Rose's hair as he searched for injuries. But…

She just had a few scratches. Nothing too terrible. Nothing that should have made Rose stay unconscious this way. She was a vamp. Vamps were strong. Too strong for this.

"Help…me…" It was the blond bastard, groaning and waking in the SUV.

Julian didn't look at him. "Rose." He'd said her name, roughly, demandingly, but his touch was tender as he stroked her cheek. "Wake up."

She didn't.

Why the hell not?

Icy tendrils seemed to snake around his heart. Fear. He didn't usually experience fear. Emotions were for the weak, and he didn't have time to waste on them. But with Rose, it was different. With Rose, everything was different.

He pulled her into his arms once more, holding her tightly, and he turned toward his motorcycle. He'd get her to safety. She was breathing, there was no sign of deep injury…

Drugged.

He stilled, just a foot away from his motorcycle, as the truth hit him. Her unconsciousness was too deep for there to be any other explanation.

"Don't…leave me…" The human yelled from the wreckage. "My legs are t-trapped! Get me out!"

Julian stared down at Rose's face. He walked forward, then he very carefully put her on the ground near his motorcycle. "I'll be right back." His hand lingered on her cheek.

"Fucking help me!"

The human was getting on his last nerve.

Julian stalked back toward the wreckage. He leaned into the open passenger side—

"Thank God," the blond gasped. "Thought you were going to *leave* me here."

"I am." Because he'd just caught sight of the syringe on the floorboard. He bent and scooped it up. Broken and empty. "What did you give her?"

"Get me out! Don't you smell the gas? Don't you —"

Julian grabbed the guy's arm. "You drugged her. Were you part of that team in the alley? Were you there for her all along?" Because the club was an obvious place to hunt for a vampire. With drinks flowing so heavily, with people dancing and getting lost in the moment — a club like that one was practically a dream vampire destination. And a vampire hunter would have known that. *You just waited there, didn't you, hoping that the vamp in the area would come in...*

The answer was on the man's face. "Get me out." Now he was pleading. "And I'll tell you everything."

A siren shrieked in the distance. The woman he'd sent away — she'd probably called the cops. He sighed. Humans. Always asking for more trouble.

"You drugged her." He didn't need any other explanation. "That was your mistake."

Fire ignited near the back of the vehicle, flames shooting up into the air.

The human screamed. *"Get me out now!"*

"Looks like someone is about to burn." He smiled. "Like I said, you made a mistake." Then Julian left the bastard. He went back to Rose, ignoring the man's screams. She was still out cold, dammit.

The blond roared. "Get me out — and I'll tell you everything I know!"

Julian stared down at Rose.

Her lashes began to flutter. His lips parted as he crouched before her. "Come on. Come back to me." He let his claws slide out and he raked his forearm, a deep enough cut that blood trickled to the surface. Then he gave Rose that blood, knowing it would help heal her.

At first, she didn't drink.

The sirens grew louder. The scent of smoke and the crackle of flames were louder.

"He has a muse! She's locked up! A muse and an angel!"

Rose's lips pressed to Julian's forearm. She began to drink. The icy tendrils finally released his heart.

"He's got a witch locked up, too! The guy wanted a mermaid, but he didn't get her. The vampire is next on his list — he wants her because she wasn't bitten or born, but created from magic. Oh, shit, dammit, the flames are almost on me! Get me out! Get me out!"

Rose's green eyes were open. She pushed his arm away, frowning. "Julian?"

The human screamed again — this time, the cry was ripe with pain.

"He's burning." Julian didn't move. "Do you want him to live or die?"

Horror flashed on her face. "*Live.*"

Because she was still a human at heart. She didn't get that some monsters were better off dead. After the hell she'd been through, he'd thought she would have learned that particular dark truth by now.

"Only for you," he said then he leapt away from her. If it had been his call alone, that wanker would have burned. In seconds, Julian was back at the SUV. He crawled through the passenger side. The flames ate at his arm, burning the forearm he'd offered to her moments before. Then he was shoving against the steering wheel, freeing the worthless bastard who'd hurt Rose. Julian dragged the guy out of the SUV, and the blond was groaning and moaning the whole damn time.

The sirens were closer now. The human cops would be arriving soon. Not much time for talking...

So he'd cut right to the chase.

He brought his claws up and shoved them against the man's throat. "Where were you taking her?"

Fear—he could smell it. The guy reeked of fear. A human who was in way over his head. "I-I was…"

"*Where.*"

"To…to a boat down on the dock. My boss…he has a boat there."

Julian let his claws cut the fool's skin. "The name of the boat." Not a question. An order.

"Th-the *Pandora.*"

Because the bastard liked to put creatures into a box? "Where are the others you mentioned?" Julian barked at him.

"I don't know, I *swear!*" The human was shaking. "I don't—"

The cops were almost there. The sirens were blasting in Julian's ears. "I have your scent. Wherever you go, I can find you now." He smiled and knew his elongated teeth would flash. His beast was far too close to the surface. "Never make the mistake of going near Rose again. If you do, I'll rip the flesh from your body."

"Julian…" Rose's soft voice. "We…we need to leave."

He dropped the human. Just let him fall into a pile of waste on the ground. Then he turned toward Rose. *Now she's ready to leave with me. Good choice, love. Good choice.* Rose was on her feet, but she was trembling—not the hard shakes of the human, but small tremors that rocked her body. He caught her hand in his, and his fingers smoothed over her wrist, a delicate caress that seemed second nature to him.

He pulled her toward the motorcycle. He got on and brought the engine snarling to life. She stood beside the bike, staring at him, her eyes so big and deep.

If a man had a soul, he could get lost in eyes like hers.

But Julian had traded his soul already.

Traded it for her.

The wind caught her thick, red hair, tossing it around her face. His fingers itched to brush it back. *Control your shit, man. Focus.*

"Get on," he ordered her as his hands curled around the handlebars. "I'm not in the mood to deal with the cops."

She glanced back at the human. "Simon…"

Was that the bastard's name?

She bit her lower lip — a full, plump lip. She had such a gorgeous mouth. *She* was gorgeous. Heart-shaped face, killer cheekbones, and a body made for pleasure. Damn, but he'd missed her.

Rose brushed back a lock of hair that blew toward her eyes. "Are we going to just leave Simon Lorne here?"

Yes, they absolutely were. If *Simon* was smart, he'd high tail it far away from the Keys. "Get on," Julian gritted again. "Simon's boss may have reinforcements coming. He wants you in the *collection.*" Something that would happen over his dead body.

He could see the flash of police lights. They'd run out of time.

Rose slid onto the motorcycle behind him. Her legs pressed against his and her arms wrapped around him.

About time. "Hold tight," he told her. "Because it's going to be one hell of a ride."

Then he took off, racing into the night, and the sirens screamed after them.

***

"Sir, sir are you all right?"

Did he look fucking all right? Simon Lorne squinted up at the cop above him. Blood was dripping in his eyes. His forehead had slammed into the steering wheel on impact, and broken glass had rained into the car.

"Need…ambulance." Something that should be obvious. That freak had cut his throat, and Simon had burns on his arms.

"It's coming. Just stay still. Help will be here soon."

Not soon enough. The vampire was gone — taken away by that bastard on the bike. The bastard with the claws and with the promise of death in his eyes. Simon couldn't even hear the roar of the motorcycle any longer.

The EMTs arrived a while later. Fucking finally. They loaded him onto a stretcher. Put him in the back of the ambulance. Then they started hooking him up to tubes—an IV and some other kind of monitor. They wrapped his burns. They bandaged his neck.

"Didn't realize...she had a protector," he said as he stared straight up.

The EMT—a pretty brunette—frowned at him as she leaned into his line of sight. "Sir?"

The ambulance lurched forward, leaving the scene.

The brunette was in the back with him. A man—thin, balding—worked at her side.

"Rose having a protector...that makes it...harder..." So much harder.

The brunette leaned closer to him. "Sir? I think you're confused."

No, he was very, very focused. He had to get back to the top of his game, and a pit stop at the hospital wasn't going to help him. Science never helped.

Magic did.

His hand flew out and locked around her throat. "Harder," he allowed. "His presence will definitely make things harder, but not impossible."

Before the woman could scream, he snapped her neck.

CHAPTER THREE

"Stop the bike!" Rose yelled. She tightened her hold on Julian. He'd driven for miles, and he hadn't spoken a word to her during that ride. She had no idea where he was taking her or what he planned, but she wasn't just going to disappear into the dark.

He didn't stop.

How typical of him.

Eyes narrowing, she leaned even closer to him. "Stop the bike, Julian," she said, nearly purring the words into his ear. She wasn't sure if a compulsion would work on another paranormal creature—she'd actually never *tried* to work her power on someone like him—but she figured she had nothing to lose.

Only the guy just kept driving.

Her breath blew out in a huff as the wind whipped against her. Fine, if that was the game he wanted to play...

He didn't have on a helmet. Neither did she. No helmet, no leather jacket. He had on a t-shirt, and the back of his neck was exposed to her.

Truly, in that instance, what was a hungry vamp to do, but take a bite?

Rose leaned forward. She put her mouth to his neck. Her lips feathered over his skin, then her tongue slid out and lightly licked him.

The motorcycle jerked to the left.

Then Julian was braking the bike. Swearing up a storm, but braking and then he whirled to face her on the motorcycle. Their faces were close, their mouths just inches apart.

"What in the hell kind of game are you playing?" His voice was a low, dangerous growl. "I pulled your sweet ass from one wreck tonight. Are you in the mood for a second?"

"My kiss distracts you enough for a wreck?" She let her brows climb. "Interesting. Now I certainly do wonder what my bite would have done."

But, before he could reply, she jumped from the motorcycle. All she'd wanted was for him to stop and she'd gotten what she wanted. Now to get away from him as fast as she—

His hand flew out and locked around her wrist. Stupid lightning-fast shifter reflexes.

"Love, you've been around humans for so long that you've forgotten just how strong others paranormals can be."

Rose's chin notched up. "Not like that whole forced close-proximity to humans bit was my choice." None of the madness ever had been—

that was the problem. "I didn't ask to get kidnapped by some covert government group and tossed in a cage." But that was exactly what had happened to her. She'd spent the last few months in hell. Oh, sure, the government had a cool name for the group that had taken her — Operation Night Switch. And the group had liked to peddle some BS about using paranormals to make the world a better, safer place.

But she'd seen nothing *better*. She'd just learned more about betrayal and pain. Because that twisted group that had kept her for so long? The bastards who'd starved her and tortured her as they tried to turn her into the perfect weapon for Uncle Sam? The group had been headed by her own brother.

A brother who was now dead. *The last of my family...gone.* And she'd felt only relief when he died. "I just got my freedom," she said, her gaze dropping to her wrist. He wasn't hurting her with his grip. Julian had never physically hurt her. "So why are you so hell-bent on taking it away?"

"Believe it or not, I'm trying to protect you."

Not. Her gaze rose to meet his. His golden stare blazed with the power of his panther.

"Consider me your paranormal protection, sweets. I've been assigned as your twenty-four, seven bodyguard. My job is to make sure that you don't wind up in a prison again."

Being caged again was the last place she intended to be.

"You think I don't know that you hate being near me?" His voice had gone rougher, and he gave a bitter laugh. "Trust me, I get it. You see me and you see pain."

That hadn't always been the case. Once, she'd looked at him and thought she saw her future waiting. But that future was long gone. Now she just had blood and death to look forward to for the next millennia.

Provided, of course, she could manage not to get thrown into another cell.

Since becoming a vampire, she'd learned some bitter lessons.

Lesson One. Trust no one. *Absolutely* no one. Because even family would turn on you in an instant. You weren't human any longer, so people tended to treat you like a monster.

Lesson Two. The paranormal world was all about survival of the fittest. The older a paranormal being was, the more powerful he or she was, too. And since Rose was a newbie, she tended to measure up terribly low on the power scale.

"Has the drug worn off?" Julian asked her.

"I'm a little sluggish, but otherwise okay." She was low on the power scale, but Julian…he was a different beast, literally. He'd been born a paranormal, so he'd been accumulating power since before he could even talk. And the stories she'd heard about him since her transformation…

He's the right hand of the devil. The instrument of death.

She'd never known him at all.

Rose licked her lips. "Why…why is Simon after me?" A shiver slid over her skin. "Is he connected to Operation Night Switch?"

His jaw hardened. "I think dumbass Simon is just the errand boy for another player on the paranormal scene. His boss is a guy who calls himself the 'Collector'. My…source told me that the Collector had been using the ONS. Getting their men to help him find certain paranormals, only he had no intention of working with Uncle Sam. The guy wanted these paranormals for his own purposes. He found them, caught them, and locked them away." His fingers stroked along the inner line of her wrist. "And he wants *you* now."

That was so not good. "For his collection." Because Julian had mentioned that before, back at the crash scene. Before he could speak, she gave a hard shake of her head. "I can't do that again. I-I can't be starved and locked away." *Tortured.* Tears stung her eyes so she blinked them away. "It won't happen."

"No, it fucking won't. Because I won't *let* it happen."

She wanted to believe him, but that just led right back to that pesky trust situation between them. Or rather, the whole *lack* of trust situation.

"I figure the best way to keep you safe is to find the Collector and cut off his head." He smiled and she saw that his canines looked extra…deadly. His teeth changed when his beast was close. Got a whole lot sharper. Sharper than even her vamp fangs because a panther had a seriously strong bite. "Since the guy is just waiting down at the dock on the *Pandora*," Julian added grimly, "that was where I was heading. You know, before you decided to play a little game of Turn-On-The-Beast."

She hadn't been playing a game. And she *hadn't* been trying to turn him on. "This Collector…he has others trapped." She remembered that part. When she'd first woken after the crash, things had been a bit blurry, but she swore she could remember someone talking about…

A muse?

A witch?

Maybe even an angel?

If demons are real, then I guess angels have to be real, too. As a human, she had been completely blind to the real world around her. The paranormals were out there, all right. Most of them hid in plain sight. The weaker ones, anyway. The stronger ones…

They stayed away from humans. Mostly because when a powerful paranormal came into contact with a human, well, the human didn't get a happy ending.

Case in point, look at my life.

"I've been told that, yes, he has others...and that dumbass who tried to take you just confirmed that to me, tonight."

She climbed back onto the motorcycle. "Then what are we waiting for?" Her hands curled around him.

He stiffened. All of that wonderful muscle went rock hard beneath her touch. "Rose?"

"You said the Collector is at the dock. Let's get our asses there, have some big showdown, and stop him." She tried to sound a whole lot more confident than she actually felt. At most moments of peril, she was utterly terrified, but Rose knew you weren't supposed to show fear in the paranormal world. Fear was a weakness.

The others preyed on the weak.

Evil — that was a strength. Don't-Give-A-Damn attitude...that was something to be admired. She was trying to fake her way through the new world she lived in.

"If he has others trapped, we have to help them." On this part, she was adamant. She'd been a prisoner, and she couldn't stand the thought that others were trapped like she'd been. *Collected.* "Come on, let's go."

His head was turned so that their eyes met. He hadn't started the bike yet. "You were trying to run from me a moment ago."

"Yes, well," she cleared her throat... *You're the biggest bad-ass I see right now. And the devil you know...he's supposed to be a whole lot better than the other monsters hiding in the dark.* At least, she hoped so. Rose pasted a bright smile on her face. "I figure the enemy of my enemy can be my temporary partner. So let's haul ass and get this done. Then you won't need to protect me any longer. I can go my own way. You can go yours."

His face hardened. "And you never have to see me again."

Her heart stuttered. "Right. Never. Never ever in the infinity that is left of my life."

His teeth snapped together. "Hold the fuck on, got it? Because I'll be going fast."

She was a vamp. She was used to super speed now. And —

He revved that engine and they raced off into the night. She held onto him tightly, her body pressed to his, and her thighs around his. The motorcycle vibrated beneath her. Rose tried *not* to notice just how good Julian felt, how strong. She tried *not* to think about how good he'd tasted.

She failed.

Soon I'll be away from him again. And soon my heart will stop hurting.

Soon...

"Drive faster," she whispered. "I can handle it." She could handle anything he threw at her.

He went even faster. She hugged him harder.

And she *hated* that they seemed to fit together so perfectly.

***

The sports yacht waited at the end of the pier. The waves were growing stronger in the distance, but the *Pandora* was tied securely and barely seemed to move in the water.

The *Pandora* was a forty-footer, one that appeared to have all of the latest bells and whistles. A faint light glowed from the yacht's interior, and Julian sure as hell hoped that his prey waited inside.

His motorcycle was hidden a few yards away. Luke Thorne actually kept a building on the dock just to store their vehicles and bikes, so Julian had stashed his ride there. Julian and Rose stalked silently toward the boat, and he made sure she stayed behind him. He didn't like the idea of her hunting with him, but he sure wasn't going to leave her alone some place. Until the Collector was dead, he planned to keep Rose at his side. That had been the deal, after all. The deal he'd made with the source who'd tipped him off about Rose being the Collector's next target.

"I don't see anyone in there," Rose whispered. Her fingers pressed to his side, and even that little touch turned him on. Did she get that? Did the woman have any fucking clue what she did to him? Probably not. Or if she did know, she didn't give a shit.

When they'd been riding on that motorcycle, and her soft body had surrounded him, he'd wanted nothing more than to pull over, take her off that bike, and take *her*. It had been far, far too long since he'd had his Rose. And even back then…back in the day when she'd still looked at him like he was some kind of hero, he'd had to use care with her. Such gentle care. A shifter wasn't supposed to take a human as a lover. Another rule he'd broken.

He'd never been good with rules.

Shifters were too rough, too wild, for human lovers. When their passions were roused, their beasts had a tendency to come out — and that meant claws. Fangs. Torn sheets. Primitive pleasure. But he'd always held tightly to his control with her. He'd held back, not wanting to so much as bruise her skin.

Because she'd been human.

Because she'd *mattered*.

She isn't human now. She can handle your beast. That meant the sex between them would be fucking insane.

Not that it was going to happen.

And that makes me all the more ready to kick some ass tonight.

"You have better hearing than I do," she continued, her voice barely a breath of sound. "Is someone on the boat? Someone I can't see?"

He did have better hearing—no other paranormal had a stronger sense of hearing than a shifter. All of his senses were enhanced—hearing, smell, vision, taste. He *felt* more. Which could be a strength or a serious weakness. "Someone is on the boat." He just didn't know if that *someone* was his intended prey or not.

Time to find out. He leveled a hard stare at Rose. "You stay behind me, every step of the way, got it?" Because maybe this was a trap. Maybe that jackass Simon had just wanted to lure him out to the *Pandora* with Rose. Maybe the guy had thought Julian would leave Rose behind on the dock while he searched the boat. Then some goons would rush to the scene and grab her.

Not happening. Wherever I go, she goes. That was the deal for the foreseeable future.

Rose sighed. "I get it. You want to lead, you want to take bullets—"

His body tensed as he remembered another time. Another place. Bullets that had torn into *her*. Hell, yes, he'd take bullets to stop her from ever suffering like that again.

"—then by all means, lead the way."

He would. And he'd go with his claws out. He rolled back his shoulders and called up his beast. His fingers changed, lengthened, as the claws sprouted from his fingertips.

"That's…always a little scary to me," she mumbled. "When you do that."

Because his claws were sharper than most knives. He gave her a grim smile. "I've always been a little scary to you." His head cocked. "But you want me anyway."

Her lips parted. He could still feel those lips on his neck. He'd gone rock hard when she put her mouth on him. The woman was seriously lucky she hadn't been in a second accident that night.

Her mouth obsessed him. Bow-shaped, red, those full lips…How many times had he fantasized about her mouth on him?

"I don't want you," she denied hotly. "Okay, wait, all I *want* is for you to get us on the boat so we can stop the bad guy. That's it. That's all."

He smiled at her. "Liar."

But they'd deal with that part, later. Right now, he needed to move fast. He probably should have killed Simon, but he'd felt…well, he'd felt *her* eyes on him and Rose asked to let the human live. So he had.

Though he fully intended to hunt down the human at the next available opportunity. Simon deserved more pain. The guy had drugged Rose.

He'd targeted her. Julian wouldn't be forgetting the guy anytime soon. *And I have his scent. That means I can track the SOB any place I want.*

They crept toward the boat. The scent of the salty ocean teased his nose. He could hear voices in the distance. Laughter. Folks were still partying at the clubs nearby. People were always partying in the Keys. They thought they were escaping from their troubles. Heading to paradise.

They had no idea that the monsters had beaten them down to the sandy shores.

He jumped onto the boat and landed easily. After all, he was cat-like for a reason. He held Rose's arm when she jumped. Not that she needed steadying. Vamps had good balance, too. He just liked holding her.

Always had.

Another weakness.

He eased down the steps that led below deck to the cabin. He could hear a faint rustle down there. A rustle and...mumbling.

"Fire...fire...Wait for Simon...Fire...Simon says...Simon says fire...Do what Simon says..."

What the fuck?

Julian kicked open the door that stood between him and his prey.

A man whirled toward him. No, not a man. More like a boy. Rail thin, with shaggy, black hair that hung into his green eyes. His hands curled at his sides as he blinked at Julian.

"N-not Simon...Simon says..."

Julian lifted up his claws. "I don't give a shit what Simon says. Tell me where the Collector is or you'll be in a whole new world of pain, kid." He hadn't heard anyone else on the boat. This kid — this sweating, mumbling kid who weirdly wore an overcoat in the freaking heat of the Keys — was his best lead.

He was...

The kid yanked open his coat. And Julian realized just why the guy was overdressed. The mumbling kid was wired to explode. *Oh, shit.*

"Julian..." Fear shook Rose's voice.

"Simon says fire...if he's not here...if he doesn't come...fire..." Terror glowed in the boy's eyes even as his fingers tightened around what Julian now saw was some kind of detonator — a trigger that was cradled in his right hand. *"Simon says..."*

Julian whirled and shoved Rose back toward the stairs. "Get out!"

"Stop him!" Rose yelled back at him. "He's just a kid! Help him, help—"

"Help..." The boy gasped out the word. *"Simon says..."*

Julian spun back toward him. Tears were raining down the boy's face.

"Can't stop...Have to do what...Simon says..."

Julian lunged for him, grabbing for that trigger.

The kid cried out, *"Sorry!"*

Julian felt Rose's fingers grab his back. *I told her to go!* But it was too late now. The kid had already pressed that trigger. Julian could hear a faint hum as the device activated. *Oh, fuck me.* But the blast hadn't ignited immediately. That meant they had time — or at least, a few precious seconds to spare.

His claws sliced right through the vest-like apparatus on the boy's torso. The bomb dropped to the floor. The hum became a beep. Julian caught the kid by the nape of his neck and threw him at Rose. *"Get him out!"*

The explosion erupted, the flames shooting out behind him, throwing him into the air, sending him hurtling toward Rose. He saw the terror in her eyes.

Then he saw the flames, surrounding them. Going for her.

Flames can kill a vampire. "No!" Julian roared.

But it was too late. The flames were too hot.

The fire came for him. He kept running for Rose even as the flames burned his skin.

The fire came for him…and for her.

CHAPTER FOUR

The water was cold. Wonderfully, perfectly cold. Cold and dark. Rose kicked up and broke the surface, sucking in a deep gulp of air.

Only she hadn't exactly come up alone.

A certain panther shifter had his arm wrapped tightly around her stomach—his hold was pretty much a death grip.

"Take another breath," he growled at her, water streaming from his dark hair. "Again, love. Fucking *again*."

And her starved lungs greedily drew in the air. As soon as she had that second breath, his lips crashed down on hers. He kissed her wildly, desperately, and the need she'd tried to push down so deep inside of herself flared to life. She wanted—

His mouth tore from hers. "Thought you were burning in front of me."

She'd thought the same thing. But…

She smiled at him even as she kicked to tread water. "Thank goodness for super speed." Because as the fire had raged all around them, consuming everything in sight like a hungry beast, she'd hauled ass up those stairs. *And* she'd grabbed her panther by the wrist on her way up.

Wait. Stop the thought. He is not your anything. Get that straight.

"Goodness…right. That's what we should thank." But his lips had twisted.

"Are you…are you hurt?" Her voice was husky and she didn't know if that was because of the all smoke and flames that had been on the boat or because she had a weird urge to seduce the guy.

"Few burns. They're already healing."

Right. Shifters healed so fast.

"What about you?"

She was staring at his mouth again. Adrenaline had her feeling shaky. Adrenaline and maybe desire. "Fine." A few blisters. Nothing that wouldn't heal.

"Good, that's—"

"*Help me!*"

Her gaze jerked to the right. The *Pandora* was there—and still burning quite brilliantly. Flames were shooting into the sky and probably attracting all sorts of attention. And that desperate, terrified "*Help me!*" cry had come from beside the boat.

Only…

The guy who'd uttered that cry had just slipped below the water's surface.

And Julian was simply treading water with her and watching the fellow drown.

Fine. I'll save him myself. She surged toward the human, but Julian pulled her back. "No way. We're getting out of here before this place becomes a circus scene." He began swimming *away* from the dock. And away from the drowning human.

"We're helping him!" She shoved against Julian, but he didn't let her go. When it came down to a battle of strength, unfortunately, his trumped hers.

Damn shifters.

"Julian, no, he's just a kid!" He was a kid who had disappeared beneath the surface of the water and who had *not* resurfaced.

"He's the bastard who just tried to kill us both," Julian snapped back. He kept swimming and dragging her away from the burning boat and the dying boy.

Not a boy. He was probably around eighteen. Maybe nineteen. And he'd looked so scared on the Pandora.

"You have got to stop trying to save people who want you dead," he continued, not even sounding a bit out of breath. As if they hadn't just hurtled out of a burning boat and dropped into the ocean. "That's just gonna come back and bite you in the ass if you don't."

Her heart slammed into her ribs — and she slammed her elbow into Julian. He grunted, as if surprised, but his hold didn't loosen.

"He's dying!"

Julian stopped swimming. His gaze met hers. "He was going to kill you. That means to me…he *is* dead."

But she shook her head. *We're wasting time…time that human doesn't have.* "You cut the bomb off him. You were trying to save him. You might pretend to be some heartless bad-ass, but you're not. You saw a terrified kid, same as me, you saw — "

He jerked her even closer, smashing her body against his. "I was trying to cut through the wires and stop the bomb, not save the jackass."

She blinked. Was that true?

"I am a heartless bad-ass. You need to remember that shit." His jaw hardened. "Now we're getting the fuck out of here. This place was a trap. I need to regroup and figure out what the hell is happening."

"I can't leave him." It was her human side talking, the side she hadn't been able to kill. The side others hadn't been able to kill, either. "Please, Julian, just get him out of the water. Or let *me* go so I can get him. I'll make a deal with you." Her words tumbled out because the kid was *gone.* Sinking to a watery grave. "I'll give you anything you want, just — "

"Deal," he said flatly.

And just like that, he let her go.

He sank beneath the water, seeming to drop like a stone. One moment, he was there. The next, he was just gone. She spun around, looking for him, then she dove under the water, heading toward the general direction that she *thought* the human was in. The water was dark and murky, and there were no stars out, there was only the waves, only the ocean stretching and —

Julian's eyes. Julian's glowing, golden eyes.

He was in front of her. And he had the human. Julian caught her wrist and they kicked toward the surface. Then they were moving — so fast. She used her own speed and strength to help Julian. They didn't swim back to the dock, but instead they traveled to a small beach just a bit down the shoreline. Julian carried the boy out, and the fellow wasn't moving. He hung like a rag doll in Julian's arms. Julian dumped the boy on the beach.

"A deal is a deal."

She scrambled toward the human. Was he even breathing? She put her fingers to his throat. Rose didn't feel a pulse. She put her ear next to his mouth. There was no stir of air. And he felt so cold. God. They'd gotten him too late.

She started CPR, pushing down with her compressions. She'd just counted her tenth compression when —

He choked up air. *Yes!* He choked and sputtered and seemed to vomit out water as he turned onto his side. He was alive. They'd saved him and—

And Julian already had his claws at the kid's throat.

"Julian, seriously, give the guy a minute." But she kept her voice low. They weren't *that* far from the flames. Other humans were over there. She could hear their voices. It wasn't as if folks could just ignore flames shooting into the sky— that show had attracted plenty of attention.

And attention was a bad thing in the paranormal world.

"Who are you?" Julian's voice was cold and hard as he glared at the kid.

The human trembled.

"I don't ask questions twice." His claws cut into the guy's skin. "Remember that."

"F-Francis Haddow…" He licked his lips. "Friends…call me Frankie."

"Do I look like I'm your fucking friend?"

Francis shook his head.

"Why the hell did you try to kill yourself *and* us?"

Francis's eyes ballooned. "What? No!" His body trembled. "No, no, I—"

Julian yanked him up and pointed toward the flames. "You see that big ball of fire over there? *You* did that, mate. You set off a bomb on the *Pandora*. You nearly killed yourself and you tried to take us to hell with you."

"*OhmyGod*." Francis shuddered. He couldn't seem to stop shuddering. "No, no, *no*. I was just at a bar, I used my fake ID, I got inside and then…" His eyes squeezed shut. "I don't know what happened, I swear, I don't *know!*"

"You were mumbling your *'Simon says'* bullshit constantly and now you want me to buy that you don't remember—" But Julian broke off. Then he swore. A lot. And his British accent got thicker.

A sign that wasn't good. She'd learned that. Usually, his accent just flowed lightly beneath his words—like when he called her love. But when he went all clipped with his voice…she knew that meant trouble.

"Nice one, you dodgy bastard." Julian glared at the flames in the distance. "Nice one."

Uh, from where she was standing, there was nothing *nice* about it.

Julian pulled the human up by the scruff of his neck. "You're coming with us, Francis."

"No!" Francis was almost yelling. A bad thing considering they didn't want to attract any attention. "I'm going home." He tried to run.

Rose winced because she knew that plan wasn't going to work out for him.

It didn't. Francis made it maybe two feet before Julian's fist plowed into his face…and down Francis went. He was out completely.

She crossed her arms over her chest and glowered at Julian. "Did you *have* to knock him out?"

"Absolutely." Water still dripped down Julian's body. His shirt clung to his chest like a second skin. He scooped up Francis as if the kid weighed nothing and threw him over his shoulder. "Can't have him running, not when I need more answers."

She rather wanted answers, too.

"Come on," Julian said as he strode down the small beach. "I've got a friend nearby. He'll take us to safety for the night."

Safety. She could use a bit of that. But… "Exactly where is this safe house?"

"You're not going to like the answer."

"I like very little about this night."

He kept walking. "It's Luke's house."

Her eyes squeezed closed. *Luke. Luke Thorne.* Luke…AKA *the Lord of the Dark.* The guy who controlled every dark paranormal creature in the world. She was pretty sure he might just be the devil, but she'd always been too afraid of the man to actually ask that question. She did know certain very scary facts about the Lord of the Dark.

He was the most powerful dark paranormal being in the world. No question. Period.

And he'd been able to bring her back from the dead. He'd used some kind of black magic to turn her into a vampire.

The third thing she knew about him? He terrified her.

"I'm not going to Luke's place." He had an island nearby. His own private slice of paradise — or, well, hell considering what he was. Luke didn't like to be near the humans so he generally kept to himself. And woe be unto the person who tried to disturb his sanctuary. "I *can't* see him."

"Relax." He'd stopped walking, just for a moment. "Luke isn't there. He's gone with his lady love. He and Mina vanished to an undisclosed location for the next few weeks. They wanted some quality time. You don't have to worry about him."

Had he seriously just said Luke had a "lady love" right then? And that the guy had jetted away for quality time? "He can't love anyone."

Now Julian looked back at her. "You think because someone is called…evil…by the rest of the world…you think that automatically means the person can't love?"

When it came to Luke, yes. She did believe that. Rose nodded.

"He'd die for Mina. He'd give up all his power in an instant — for her." He stared at Rose.

"Even the most powerful beings have weaknesses."

She glanced toward the flames. Fire. That was her weakness. Luke had been the one to warn her that if she ever burned to ash, she was dead, forever.

"Let's go. The boat is close by and I am done with this fucking night." He turned once more.

And she found herself hurrying after him. He was her paranormal protection, right? So she'd stay close, for the moment.

Besides, she didn't exactly trust him *not* to hurt the human. Julian could be unpredictable, thanks to his beast side. If he was going to interrogate Francis, she intended to be there. Someone had to keep the panther in check.

They walked in silence for a time, until they approached what she thought was a private house. Only Julian didn't go into the house. Instead, he headed for the dock behind it.

"Marcos!" Julian's voice rang out. "Get the boat going, *now*."

A man appeared, rushing out to untie the boat. Her gaze darted to the side of the vessel. *Devil's Prize*. Oh, jeez…that had to be Luke's boat.

Julian jumped onboard and dropped the human onto the deck. He just let Francis fall with a thud. "Probably going to need to tie him up," he muttered as he studied the human with narrowed eyes. "Marcos, toss me some extra rope."

And the guy did—no questions asked. Marcos just tossed the rope to Julian as if it were a normal thing to basically kidnap a person.

Rose bit her lip as she stood on the wooden dock.

"Marcos." Julian was tying up Francis, not looking at her as he spoke. "The lady hesitating over there and looking all judgmental is Rose. She's coming back to the island with us."

Marcos gave her a quick, searching glance.

"And Rose, this is Marcos." He tied a quick knot, then nodded, as if satisfied. "Marcos is ex-Navy, and he's the all-around best captain in the Keys." Julian ran his hand through his hair, sending droplets of water flying. "Now, the introductions are done, so let's get the hell out of here."

Rose exhaled and jumped onto the boat. As soon as her feet touched the deck, Julian was there. His hands wrapped around her body to steady her. Not that she needed steadying.

"Good choice," he whispered, and she felt his breath stir against her ear. She would *not* shiver.

She shivered. Dammit. "I didn't realize I had a choice. You said I had to stay with you. Twenty-four, seven, right? Weren't those your words?"

He was wet. But warm. Always warm.

"Yeah, those were my words." He smiled. "But you could have run again. Made me chase you." He...nuzzled her.

Seriously, that was what he'd just done. Nuzzled her neck as if he were giving her some kind of panther caress.

Then he let her go.

"But if I'd chased you, that would have just brought out the beast in me." He stared at her with his glowing eyes. "It's better if he comes out when we're alone. Not here."

Rose swallowed. "Julian..."

The boat was already moving.

Julian turned his back to her. "Don't forget..."

Her hands twisted nervously in front of her.

"I've already kept up my part of the deal. Your turn will come soon."

She knew he'd just given her a warning.

CHAPTER FIVE

He wasn't surprised to find Rayce Lovel waiting on the island's dock. The wolf shifter would have heard the boat's approach, and Rayce — being Rayce — would have come down to see just what was happening.

After all, Rayce and Julian had both been left to guard the island in Luke's absence. If anything happened to the place while their buddy was gone, there would truly be hell to pay.

"Didn't expect to see you back so soon," Rayce called out. His blond hair glinted beneath the light on the dock. "Poor hunting night?" Then his gaze darted to Rose — a very quiet Rose. "Or perhaps, a very, very good hunting night?"

Julian growled. He didn't like the way Rayce eyed Rose. The wolf needed to tone that shit down.

"Why do wet women keep being brought to this island? Not that I'm complaining," Rayce added as he caught the line that Marcos threw to him. "Quite the contrary. I just — "

"Get the human off the boat. He needs to be taken into containment until morning." Francis had woken up on the ride out to the island. His terror had turned into screams — screams that had stopped when Julian gagged the fellow. "I am not in the mood to deal with him now."

No, what he needed right then…it was a run. A wild, fast and furious run across the island. He had to let his beast out. Too much had happened that night —

Two times. Two fucking times death tried to take Rose.

His control was razor thin. The beast demanded his freedom, and the man wasn't going to be able to hold him back much longer.

"A bound and gagged human?" Rayce bounded onto the boat and eyed the kid. "Definitely an interesting hunting night."

Julian grunted. "I think he was under a compulsion. He doesn't seem to remember jack shit right now, but I am hoping with the right…tools…" Tools the human would *not* like. "With the right tools, I'm hoping that will change."

Rayce easily slung Francis over his shoulder. "I know just the cell for him."

Because, yes, Luke's island paradise came complete with its own prison. Luke truly believed in being prepared.

But before Rayce could leave the boat, Rose stepped into his path. "He's a kid, okay? Not some prisoner. He doesn't belong in a cell. He's confused and scared and he has no idea what's happening." Her words tumbled out, fast and husky. And...shaking. "You can't just lock him up. You can't hurt him."

They could. "The cell is for his protection, Rose. Rayce and I aren't the only monsters on the island right now."

At that one word—monsters—she flinched. Then she turned the full force of her big, green eyes on him. "Locking him up...how does that make us better than the ONS? How does that make us any better than—than this Collector guy that you keep worrying me about?"

"It doesn't make us better." He'd never said he *was* better and, hell, he was almost out of time. He could feel his muscles jerking and stretching. In just a few moments, he'd be doing a full-on shift right in front of her. He didn't want her to see that.

Shifts weren't pretty. They were brutal and they were vicious and, sometimes, if he wasn't very, very careful...his panther could take over completely.

There was a reason he had no pack to call his own. A reason he'd gone rogue long ago.

He was a killer. Someone who could never be trusted. Especially not around humans. Especially not around…

Someone like her.

I knew that from the beginning, but I couldn't stay away from her.

"Take Rose to the main house," he ordered Rayce.

Rayce just lifted his brows. "What? Do I look like some errand boy to you? Drag the human…" he muttered as he turned away, heading up the winding path that led to the house. "Get the girl. Do all my shit for me because I'm Julian and I can't handle—"

"*Rayce.*"

His friend—friend, general jack-ass, trouble-maker, whatever—turned back toward him. And whatever he saw on Julian's face had Rayce tensing.

"Rose," Rayce said her name flatly. "Bring that sweet ass of yours up here with me, now."

"I don't like him," Rose muttered.

Julian clenched his hands into fists. He jumped off the boat. He had to get away from Rose. He had to get away from them all.

But Rose—she followed him. She grabbed his arm. "We aren't done, Julian! You can't just run away from me—"

"You don't want to see what happens next." His voice was rough, broken. Speech was too hard then. His bones had started to snap. In a moment, he would be on all fours, and fur would burst from his skin. He'd learned to control the shift—mostly—since coming to Luke's island so long ago. But because of that hellish night, because of all the things that had happened to Rose, there was no longer any control left for him. He was at a breaking point. The panther loved it when the man broke.

"Julian?" Concern softened her face. "Are you okay?"

He pulled from her. "Get her *away!*" Julian roared to Rayce.

Rayce kept the human over his shoulder, but he bounded toward Rose. He caught her arm. "We need to go…now. Come on, lady, *now!*"

Rayce pulled her, trying to force her up the path, and Julian whirled, trying to flee before the change hit.

But it was too late.

He could feel the burn beneath his skin. He hit the ground, landing on all fours. The snap and crunch of his bones just got louder. An itch started along his skin—and then the fur burst out, covering him. He opened his mouth, snarling with the pain because the shift wasn't gentle. He'd fought the beast too long for any gentleness. A mouthful of razor sharp teeth exploded. He became the panther, running and bounding forward. His paws hit the earth. His claws were ready to rip and kill and, helplessly, he looked toward Rose once more.

Only to see her staring at him in horror.

But then, that was the way she usually looked at him.

Some things never fucking change.

***

"Well…" the man next to her drawled. "That was a little awkward, huh?"

More than awkward. "I didn't realize it hurt him so much." His pain had been unmistakable. The sound of crunching bones would haunt her.

"Not like it's easy to completely reshape into another being. When the fire of the shift burns through you, there are only two choices. Fight it and let it hurt worse. Or give in…and still let it hurt like a bitch." He hoisted Francis higher onto his shoulder. The human was twitching, but not struggling…much. "There's not exactly any winning way to do it."

The panther—a big, black panther with seriously scary teeth—had vanished. Rose cleared her throat. "You sound like you're speaking from experience."

"I am."

Her gaze jerked toward him. When he smiled at her, she saw that his canines were a little too long. A little too sharp. His face shape had altered a bit, too, becoming more angular. His eyes—a green brighter than her own—seemed to shine. "You're a...panther?"

"Hell, no." He turned and headed up the path. "I'm a wolf, baby. Pure blood wolf. The baddest of the bad."

She glanced back toward the woods. The island was freaking huge—sandy beaches, thick woods, dense vegetation. The perfect playground for shifters. The panther had gone into the woods. Maybe...should she follow him? Rose took a step in that direction.

"Don't even think it," the wolf shifter called back to her. "Because that is just asking for trouble. Julian's beast is in control and if he were to hurt you while the panther was ruling..." He stopped and seemed to consider things. "That wouldn't be pretty."

A cold chill swept over her. "I thought he stayed in control when he was a panther. That the man was always inside, guiding the beast." So *maybe* she'd tried to learn about shifters. Her curiosity had been more than justified, given her history.

"Not tonight. I could see it. His control was gone." He gave a low whistle. "Which totally begs the question...just what happened tonight?"

She bit her lip and decided that, okay, perhaps going into the woods after a panther wasn't going to be her best plan. Rose turned and headed up the path. "Someone drugged me. And then there was a fire." She winced. "A bomb. It blew up the boat we were searching on, and we barely got off the thing alive." That explosion and her near-death experience had been way too close for comfort. "Uh, who exactly, are you, by the way?"

"Right. No official introduction, huh?" He kept moving. "My name's Rayce Lovel."

He was nearly as tall as Julian, and he had wide shoulders. But where Julian had dark hair — nearly perfect black — Rayce had thick, curling blond hair. And he just moved with an easy, almost carefree stride. He was teasing her, laughing, and…he just didn't *seem* evil.

But then, he was carrying a bound and gagged human over his shoulder.

She didn't speak again until they were in the house. House, mansion, prison…whatever. It was Luke's domain. A massive structure that reeked of money. She stood in the foyer, glancing down at the marble beneath her feet. At least she wasn't dripping on it, that was a plus, but her bare feet were leaving a muddy trail.

When had she lost her shoes? When she'd first gone into the water off Key West? She hadn't even noticed they were missing until that moment.

"Be right back. Just going to get our guest settled…" Rayce marched down the hallway, but he paused and glanced back at her. "You should really just stay right...*there* until I get back. Don't go exploring on your own, okay? Not exactly a safe plan."

Then he was gone.

"Don't hurt Francis!" Rose yelled. "He's just a kid!" A kid who truly had seemed to be under a compulsion, just as Julian had mentioned.

Simon says...

She wrapped her arms around her body. The way Francis had been talking on the *Pandora*, it had certainly sounded as if Simon had been the one to give him the orders. But...Simon had been a human, right?

Just an errand boy for the Collector?

He'd seemed human.

Or had he been something more?

A big, spiral staircase led up to the next level of the house. She paced toward it and her hand reached out to slide against the smooth banister. The house felt massive. It also felt cold. Empty. Hardly a home—more like a fortress. But, really, what else would she expect from Luke? He wasn't exactly Mr. Warmth.

"The human is safe for the night."

She jumped. Rose had supernatural senses, but the wolf had just snuck up on her. She whirled around, heart racing, and found him standing just a few feet away.

"All snug and safe," Rayce continued dryly. "I even gave the kid some food." His brows lifted. "And people say werewolves are heartless."

"Who…who says that?"

He tapped his chin. "Wait. Maybe the saying is that we take *out* hearts. Just slice them right out of our prey's chests." He shrugged. "I always get that one confused."

She blinked.

He smiled. A dimple flashed in his cheek. He looked friendly. Harmless. Like some All-American athlete-type who should be on a cereal box.

Only he'd just talked about cutting the heart from a person's body.

Not so All-American.

She tucked a lock of hair behind her ear. "When will…when will Julian be back?"

"Miss him already?"

Her eyes narrowed at his mocking tone.

But Rayce just smiled. "Why don't you go get some rest?" He pointed to the side, down another snaking hallway. "Take the third door to the right. Use that room. When dawn comes, Julian should be back to his normal self. Sometimes, you just need to let your beast out."

She didn't move. "And that's what he's doing…letting his beast out?"

"I think it was more that his beast took over. Happens, you know. The primitive side wins."

Rose bit her lip and glanced toward the front door. "I think I'll wait out there for him to come back."

Rayce laughed—a deep, booming sound. She didn't like his laugh.

Her gaze swung back toward him.

His laughter slowly faded, but he was still smiling as he said, "Julian's little vampire…"

Rose stiffened. "I'm not his anything."

Rayce stalked toward her.

She backed up. A habit. When an unknown paranormal approached, she had a tendency to flee. She retreated until her back hit the table that was against the foyer wall. A vase wobbled behind her, and Rayce's hands flew out, catching it before the vase could crash. Catching it—and trapping her with his body.

"Don't want to piss off Luke," he murmured. "That is a seriously bad mistake." He put the vase back into position. His hands slid back to his sides, but he didn't move away from her. "Getting on the Lord of the Dark's bad side is never a good plan."

"I shouldn't be here." She should be living a nice, safe, *normal* life far away from this madness. She shouldn't have spent months being tortured and starved. She shouldn't always be so afraid.

"Where should you be, little vamp?" His voice had changed, gone soothing.

And that just scared her even more.

"I don't want to be like this. I want to go back to the way things were before."

"Before?"

"Before Luke Thorne changed me."

He absorbed that but still stared at her quizzically. "Would it be better to go back *before* you met Julian?"

In the distance, she could have sworn that she heard a roar. Rose jumped.

Rayce sighed. "You're a vamp now. There *is* no going back. And instead of being afraid, you need to make all of the other paranormals fear *you*. That's the way it is in our world. Strength is prized. Weakness is used." His expression hardened. "You don't want to be used."

She wanted *out* of there. Her gaze darted toward the front door once more.

"Julian isn't the only beast running wild on the island. Plenty of others are out there. You don't want to tangle with them. Very, very bad mistake."

She swallowed. "Who else is here?"

He took a step back. "Oh, you know, the worst of the worst. The dark paranormals that only Luke can keep in check. You make a deal with him, he owns your soul for a time…basic shit."

"I never made a deal with him." She'd never asked for any of this. She'd never —

"You didn't need to. Julian traded for you. Blood and death and pain...so that you wouldn't die."

His words made her heart ache. Rose shook her head.

He growled. Anger thickened that guttural sound.

She stopped shaking her head.

"I don't have many friends," he said, his voice still deep and rumbling. "And don't fucking tell Julian that I consider him to be one."

Uh, okay.

"But he has walked through *hell* for you. And you are still afraid of him." His lips twisted in disgust. "I don't get it. He's always held himself back when he's with you. You're probably the safest person on earth when he's near. You're the *only* one he'll never turn his claws on. Don't you get that? Don't you see?"

"You don't understand..."

"No, *you* don't. You're still clinging to your human hope. Let that shit go. Vamp up. Get your undead life together and throw the guy a bone." He raked a hand over his face. "Do you have any clue how many people he has killed, *for you?*"

Her heart nearly stopped. "What?"

The front door flew open and slammed against the wall. She didn't scream — good for her. She did whirl toward the door and she saw a naked Julian standing there. His muscles bulged, his golden eyes blazed, and his claws were currently gripping the door frame.

"Shut…up…wolf," he gritted out, each word sounding like a struggle.

Rayce let out a long sigh. "Here we go…"

Julian shoved away from the door frame. "Your scent…is…*on* her."

"Right. I can explain that. She nearly broke a vase. I reached around her and—" He broke off. "Look, I think you need to run some more. I can still see your beast."

So could she.

Julian appeared…bigger…than before. Stronger. His face seemed carved from stone, his muscles heaved and his whole body shuddered as he stood there.

The man was fighting the beast. She could practically see it. Only…why? Why was he there? Why wasn't he still out running? He needed that. She might not fully understand the shifter life, but it was obvious his panther was fighting for freedom.

"Heard you…" His breath rasped out. "Stop…scaring her…"

And *her* breath caught in her lungs. He'd come back, transformed, because he thought Rayce was frightening her?

Okay, truth time. The wolf did scare me. I don't want Julian killing for me. I don't want anyone killing for me. She'd had enough death to last several lifetimes.

But Rose found herself sliding away from Rayce and creeping toward the door — toward Julian.

"Uh, wait, maybe don't do that right now —" Rayce very, very loudly whispered.

She shot him an irritated glare. "You just told me I was safe with him."

"He is going to change again any second. Let's not tempt fate —"

She hated fate. Fate was mean and cruel. Fate could screw off. Rose inched closer to Julian. His chest heaved as her fingers reached up, hovering over his skin. She would *not* look down at the lower part of his body.

Her gaze dipped down.

Okay, maybe she would.

Damn. Some things are even better than you remember.

Her fingers skimmed over his chest. "You said I'd be safe here."

He gave a jerky nod.

"Then I won't be afraid tonight." A little lie, but one he seemed to need.

His nostrils flared.

"Go run. Do what you need to do." *Then come back to me.* She wanted to say those words so badly, but she managed to hold them back.

His head lowered and he...he did that little nuzzle thing again. Where he rubbed his head against her neck. It was odd but sensual. She liked it. She found herself putting her arms on his shoulders. Holding him. And, surprisingly, she wasn't afraid of him. Not of the sharp teeth or the enhanced strength—not of anything about him.

She just wanted to keep holding him.

But Rayce cleared his throat. "So, yeah, you're naked and about to go all beast mode. This is the time when you need to step back."

She felt the rumble of Julian's growl.

Only...he stepped back. He stared at her a moment more, then he whirled and ran back into the night. She took a step after him, but stopped when she heard the crunch of bones. Her stomach twisted. So much pain.

She didn't like for Julian to feel pain.

"Told you," Rayce murmured, sounding pleased as hell with himself. "He *can't* hurt you. If anyone else had gone up to him right then, Julian would have sliced them right open."

Her hand lifted and her fingers trailed along the doorframe. His claws had left deep gouge marks along the wood. She traced them and her heart grew heavier in her chest. "How many people has he killed?"

"That's a question for him, not me. I already did my over-sharing part for the night." Then his hands were on her waist and he pulled her back from the doorway.

She frowned at him.

But he just gave her his slow smile. The dimple winked again. "Told you, there are plenty of other bad things out there. Let's not go drawing them in by dangling bait in front of their faces."

"So I'm bait now?"

"No, you're Julian's vamp. Thought we went over that. So if someone comes at you, he'll freak and there will be a battle I'm not in the mood to stop tonight." He nudged her toward the hallway. "Go that way. Get changed. Sleep. When you wake up, Julian will be back. Minus his more beastly side."

She took a few steps toward that hallway. Then, unable to help herself, Rose glanced back at him. "He's...talked to you? About me?"

Rayce laughed. "He's told me as little as possible."

Oh.

"But sometimes, you don't need words to see the truth. And I see how he looks at you."

Her throat went dry. "How is that?"

"Like someone who has been in hell...and just had a glimpse of paradise."

No, he was wrong. Julian did *not* look at her like that.

"Sweet dreams, vamp," Rayce said.

She turned and shuffled down the hallway. Her dreams were never sweet. They hadn't been since she'd become a vampire. She only had nightmares. Visions of herself dying — getting shot as Julian stared down at her in horror. Visions of being trapped in a tiny cell. Hunger. Pain.

Death.

No, there would be no sweet dreams for her. There never were.

She stopped in front of the third door on the right. Rose opened the door and stepped inside. Not a room, but a suite. One with heavy, cherry wood furniture. Dark, thick curtains hung over the windows. A massive, four-poster bed had been positioned right in the middle of the suite —

A bed that had claw marks on its wooden posts. Eyes widening, she rushed toward the bed. Her hand lifted and she traced the marks, just as she'd traced the ones on the door frame before.

Julian's claw marks.

Julian's room.

She turned around.

Rayce stood in the doorway. She hadn't heard him follow her. *Shifters can move way too quietly.* He was staring at her, a slightly apologetic look on his face. "Yeah, sorry about this...but I *am* going to lock you in for the night."

"What?"

"And the room has been — well, let's just say it's been enhanced so that paranormals can't get out. I mean, when Julian has his bad nights, we can't have him busting loose. So vamp strength won't help you. Julian wanted you safe for the night and that means we can't risk you running around where the wild things are. So just shower, change into one of his shirts, and have those sweet — "

"I don't have sweet dreams!" She ran for him.

He jerked the door shut before she could grab him. Rose heard the faint click of a lock sliding into place. She tried wrenching the door open. She tried slamming her body into the wood. *Vamp strength. Vamp. Strength!*

But nothing happened. Because the tricky jerk was right...there was some kind of enhancement in place. Still, she didn't give up.

She screamed and pounded against the door.

She couldn't be trapped. Not again.

She couldn't be prisoner.

Not again.

***

The pretty vampiress slammed into the door once more. Rayce winced when he felt the vibrations of the wood. "Uh, Rose? If you hurt yourself, Julian is only going to be pissed at me."

Her answer was another slam against the door.

"It's just for tonight." Maybe. He could lie easily. "I know you don't like being prisoner, okay? I heard what the ONS did to you—"

"*Let me out!*" Her shriek easily carried through the wood.

"But we're not ONS. We're not—" He actually had to catch himself there. He'd almost said *We're not the bad guys.* That would have been total bullshit. "We're not the ones trying to hurt you now." There. Much better. "I'm walking away, all right?" Rayce took a step back. "I'd suggest that you go to sleep and have—"

"*Screw your sweet dreams!*"

His lips twitched. He could really like that vamp. No wonder Julian was obsessed.

Whistling, he turned on his heel and headed down the hallway. He'd check on the human visitor and then maybe...maybe he'd go for a run, too. His wolf had been dying for a night out.

CHAPTER SIX

Julian came back to the house just before dawn. Streaks of light were starting to edge over the water as the sun rose. He'd grabbed a pair of sweats from one of the cabins nestled on the island. There were plenty of places like that set up — safe spots for shifters so that they could dress after a transformation.

He paced down the hallway and stopped before his room. Rose was in there. He could smell her. He could —

The key was still in the lock.

Fucking hell.

Rayce had *locked* her inside. He'd never told the wolf to do that! He'd just said to keep her safe! Fuck, fuck, fuck! Julian yanked at the key and shoved open the door. He bounded inside.

Rose was in the bed. She wore his shirt, a big, black t-shirt that seemed to swallow her. She was turned on her side and he could see the tear tracks on her face.

Rose didn't like to be locked up.

I am going to kill Rayce. He whirled, ready to rip the wolf apart.

"Don't lock me in again." Her voice. Soft, husky, and coated with pain.

His shoulders stiffened. "I won't, love. I swear it." He was just going to beat the ever loving hell out of a certain mangy werewolf.

He heard the rustle of the bed covers behind him and then the faint pad of her feet on the hardwood floor. Julian forced his hands to unclench as he turned toward her. "I'm sorry." The words came out stilted and felt awkward on his tongue. He didn't usually apologize to anyone or for anything, but this was different. This was Rose.

His hand lifted and he wiped away a tear that lingered on her cheek. Her lips parted. Her eyes seemed to go even greener.

"I never meant for you to be locked up." Protection was one thing. Trapping her was another.

"So I'm not your prisoner?"

"No, hell, *no.*" He should stop touching her. He wasn't. He was caressing her cheek. Her skin was like silk. "I brought you here so you could be safe. Not so some dumbass wolf could torture you. You've been hurt e-fucking-nough. It needs to stop. It *has* to stop." If he had his way, she'd never know a moment of pain again. His hand slid down her neck. A soft, tender neck. "I'll stop it."

Her head tipped back as she stared up at him. "How did we get here?"

He blinked, confused.

"I thought I'd found Mr. Right. You were tall, dark, and mysterious. I looked at you and didn't want anyone else."

He'd looked at her and, as far as Julian had been concerned — there had been no one else.

"But you were lying to me, the whole time. Pretending to be someone you weren't."

Pretending to be a human. "It wasn't damn easy." Especially when he'd had her in his bed. He'd wanted to let his wild side out, wanted that so badly, but he'd held back. For her.

Then he'd lost her anyway.

Because when I'm close to her, she always gets hurt. That's what happens to anyone who is connected to me. Pain.

He wanted more for her.

Julian cleared his throat. "I'll leave the door open, okay? I swear I will. You get back in bed and sleep for a few hours. I won't interrogate the human without you." Mostly because he needed her for the interrogation. A little vamp compulsion would help immensely. Of course, if she wasn't in the mood to lend a hand, he could always do things the old fashioned way...with his claws.

*I've hurt so many others in my life. I'm Luke's
assassin. Death is my game. Why did I ever think my
life could be different? That I could be different?*

She glanced back at the bed as his hand slid
away from her. She turned away, and he let out a
long, slow breath. Right. He had a wolf to find
and skin. He had—

Rose looked back at him. Her hand lifted.
"Will you stay with me?"

He shook his head. He'd misheard.
Absolutely imagined those quiet words. Rose
saw him as her enemy these days. No way would
she want him in bed with her.

Wishful fucking thinking.

"I just…I don't want to be alone. When the
ONS had me, I was always alone. They kept me
away from everyone else. They kept me in the
dark and I just…" Her chin lifted and her hand
fell. "Never mind. I'm not supposed to be scared.
Isn't that what everyone keeps saying? I
shouldn't be afraid. I'm supposed to be a bad-ass.
I'm evil. I'm—"

He scooped her into his arms.

Shock flashed on her face. "Julian?"

"You're not evil. Screw what others say." But
he *hated* her fear. Hated it as much as her pain.
"You be you, sweets. I've got enough evil for us
both."

A furrow appeared between her brows. He
carried her toward the bed and then lowered her

until she was nestled on the mattress. Then he stalked around to the other side of the bed and crawled in with her.

And she shocked him again. She rolled toward him. She touched *him*.

"Are you as bad as others say?"

He tucked a lock of hair behind her ear. Such a small ear. "Worse."

The furrow deepened. "I don't...you're not, though, with me."

He eased closer to her. "That's because you aren't like the others." The back of his hand trailed over her cheek. He liked touching her. Why resist something he enjoyed so much? Soon enough, she'd be far away. He'd never touch her again. "There's no death order over your head so I don't need to be bad."

Her eyes widened.

Probably the wrong thing to say.

"How many...how many people have you killed?"

"Humans?" The memories flashed in his head. "Two." He'd carry those screams forever. "Paranormals?" His lips twisted into a smile that he knew was grim. "Lost count."

She searched his gaze. "You're lying to me."

He didn't let his expression alter.

"I think you remember them all."

She didn't understand. If he remembered them all, madness would come.

"Why did you do it?"

Why did he kill? He forced a slow smile. "It's the nature of the beast." His panther was a ruthless killer. One driven by dark impulse and a hunger for blood.

Her lashes flickered. "Why didn't you let me go? Why did you get Luke to change me?"

Because I didn't want to be in a world without you. "I'm a selfish bastard." Instead of letting her go, he'd forced her into a world that she would never fit into.

Because he hadn't been lying to her...

She wasn't evil. That was the problem. She just wasn't bad enough. But he hadn't cared when he'd made his deal. He hadn't cared about any consequences. His gaze dropped to her mouth. Those perfect red lips. A mouth built for sin. A mouth that was in every one of his dreams.

But then, his dreams were usually about her.

His nightmares were about her dying.

Julian swallowed. "No more questions, okay?" Because there were some answers he didn't want to give her. "Sleep." His head dropped back against his pillow. He thought she'd move away, perhaps curl onto her side of the bed.

Rose put her hand on his chest. "If I...if I scream, just wake me up."

What?

"The nightmares always come."

Her lashes drifted closed.

Fucking hell. *He* was her nightmare, and he knew it.

He pulled the covers up over them. His eyes closed.

Her hand stayed over his heart.

***

Simon stared at the wreckage that remained of the *Pandora*. Cops were rushing around, fire fighters were still on the scene, and he was left to stand in the small crowd of humans who'd gathered at sunrise to watch the chaos.

Had the vampiress died in those flames? He'd given strict orders to young Francis. If Simon hadn't returned to the boat, then the *Pandora* had to burn.

He couldn't risk leaving evidence behind, no clues that might lead to his base.

But what happened to the vampiress? He hadn't wanted her to burn. He needed her, dammit. Finding someone else just like her would be nearly impossible. She was so necessary to his plans.

I might have just fucked myself.

His back teeth ground together. He'd wanted the big bastard to die — the freak with the claws and the too sharp teeth. A shifter? Simon figured that was what the jerk had been. He'd told him where the *Pandora* was, thinking the guy was on a rescue mission, maybe looking for the witch or the muse.

It was easy for men to become obsessed with the muse.

So he'd given up the *Pandora*, thinking the guy would go after the vessel alone but...

But I saw the way he touched her when they stood next to the motorcycle. The shifter cares for the vamp. He'd tried to yell after them, begging them to come back, but the shifter had just driven away.

Vampiress...I need you alive. Or, as alive as she *could* be.

A woman bumped into him. "Oh, sorry," she said, voice rising a bit in nervousness. "I just...I hope no one was hurt, don't you?"

He hoped his vampiress hadn't been hurt.

I need to find her. I need to figure out what happened.

His gaze darted over the human who'd had the misfortune of literally running into him. A blonde, in her mid-twenties, with sun-kissed skin. Pretty enough, he supposed.

Not that he went for pretty.

Why bother with the ordinary? He'd never enjoyed ordinary. His Helene had been perfection beyond belief once. *She will be again.*

The blonde's weak smile slipped. "Is...is everything okay?"

"Everything will be fine." He offered her his hand. He was pretty sure he'd managed to get all of the blood off his fingers. "I'm Simon."

Her smile came back. "Keri."

Then he leaned in toward her and dropped his voice, letting the power flow out. "Keri...would you like to play a little game?"

Her gaze went glassy. "Wh-what kind of game?"

"How about...*Simon Says*..."

***

Her whimper woke him. Julian's eyes jerked open at the soft sound, and he rolled toward Rose instantly.

"Love?"

She'd curled into a little ball, moving away from him. He touched her shoulder. "Rose, Rose, wake up, it's just—"

She attacked. She shot toward him and penned him to the bed. Her hands grabbed his and shoved them over his head. Her legs were on either side of his hips as she loomed over him and her bared teeth—very sharp vampire fangs—came right at his throat.

Julian didn't try to stop her. He just turned his head and gave her a better angle, offering his throat to her. He waited to feel the sting of her teeth.

"J-Julian?" Her breath blew over his neck. She didn't bite. Damn.

Rose immediately released his hands. "I'm sorry. It was a stupid nightmare. I was back in the cell, and I was so hungry, I just—"

He locked his hands around her waist before she could move away from him. "Bite me."

Her eyes widened. "What?"

"I wasn't stopping you. I fucking love it when you bite me." He stared into her eyes. "Bite me."

Her chest rose and fell. Her gaze darted to his neck. She licked her lips. Those sexy red lips.

Did she feel his arousal pressing against her? She pretty much had to feel his dick. His oversized shirt had hiked up on her, revealing the smooth expanse of her thighs. Her sex was right over his cock, and his cock was fucking huge for her right then. The second she'd climbed onto him—hell, who was he kidding? He'd fallen asleep hard for her and woken the same way. He couldn't be near Rose without wanting her.

And this was the closest he'd been to *having* her in a very, very long time.

"When I…when I bite you, I get a little out of control."

He knew that. He was counting on that. "Bite me." This time, the words were a dark order. "You said you'd do anything I wanted." His hands tightened on her waist. "I want this. I want your mouth on me." He wanted her mouth all the fuck over him, but he'd start with his throat. They could work down from there.

She swallowed and then she leaned forward. Her hair slid over his skin as her mouth pressed to his throat. But she still didn't bite him right away. She licked. She kissed.

She made his dick jerk against her.

"Rose…" Julian tried to warn her. He was only going to play nice for so long.

Her teeth sank into him.

Yes. Maybe there was a flash of pain, if so, he didn't really give a shit because the pleasure that followed was so intense. It burned right through him and he pressed his neck to her mouth, wanting her to take more. To bite harder.

Later, he planned to bite, too.

He might never have her this way again. After a nightmare, it was probably the wrong thing to do. The wrong time for seduction. A gentleman would back away.

A devil would hold her tighter.

He knew exactly what he was.

His right hand slid down her body. He caught the cotton of his borrowed shirt—he was ridiculously pleased that she'd now have his scent all over her since she'd used one of his t-shirts—and pushed it out of his way. His hand touched her silken thigh. He trailed his fingers upward.

She wasn't wearing panties.

Because, obviously, she liked to make him crazy.

His fingers slid toward her sex. Trailed slowly, giving her the chance to stop him. *But don't do that, okay, love? Just —*

She pulled her mouth from his neck.

His growl filled the air.

Her hands slammed down onto his chest. Her breath heaved out. She had the tiniest drop of his blood on her lower lip. As he stared up at her, with his hand so close to paradise, her tongue snaked out and she licked that blood drop away.

A human male might not have found the whole blood-drinking thing sexy.

He wasn't human. And he found *everything* about her to be sexy.

"I don't want you holding back," Rose whispered.

His fingers were itching to stroke her. His cock was ready to explode.

"Rayce said…" Her chin lifted. "You were holding back when you were with me. Don't do that anymore. This time…this one time, I want everything you have."

His fingers slid into heaven. She was wet and hot and he wanted to ram his cock into her and never let her go. "Be careful what you ask for, love."

Her lips parted as he stroked her. She pushed down with her hands, and her nails bit into his chest and she arched up, moaning as he stroked her.

Julian wanted her to come, just like that. With his fingers in her body and pleasure that *he* gave Rose stamped on her face. He pressed his thumb to her clit. He remembered *everything* that she liked. He'd give her that first. The soft touches. The long licks.

Then…well, once she was lost to pleasure, he'd let his beast out. He'd see if she truly could handle him now.

She was riding his hand. Lifting and lowering her body as her knees pressed into the mattress. He stroked her harder, and he put another finger inside of her. She was so freaking tight. He loved her body. Went fucking insane for her sex.

He—

Julian tumbled her back on the bed. He moved her fast, lifting her legs up and then he put his mouth on her because it had been too long since he'd tasted her. A man could only survive on a fantasy for so long before he went absolutely mad.

So he feasted. He licked and sucked and stroked with his tongue and his fingers until she was shouting out his name as she came. And he didn't give a fuck if anyone else on that island heard them. She was his—and he was going to have all of her.

"*Julian.*"

He looked up at her, her taste still on his tongue, and he knew that she'd see his beast. He could feel the power filling him. His eyes would be glowing, his cheeks hollowing, and his teeth would be sharpening.

I bite, too.

He crawled up her body. He shoved down his sweats and put the head of his cock at the entrance to her body. His claws came out then, and he didn't try to hold back the change. She wanted him? She'd get him.

He raked his claws over her borrowed shirt, and she sucked in a quick breath as he shredded the soft cotton. Just shredded the t-shirt from hem to neck. But he didn't mar her skin. Not that perfect skin. His head bent and he kissed her body. The curve of her stomach. Her belly button. Then up, up to her breasts and those tight nipples that tasted like sweet candy.

Her legs locked around his hips.

He shoved into her, a deep, hard thrust that made her gasp. Her pupils expanded, and the darkness seemed to fill her eyes. Her fangs peeked from behind her lips and she just whispered, "More."

So he gave her everything.

His claws dug into the mattress. He withdrew, then thrust deeper, slamming into her again and again. She was wet and sensitive from her release and her soft moans just drove him on. So freaking tight. So hot. Sending him out of his mind.

He couldn't get deep enough. The beast wanted so much more.

The beast was going to have her.

He caught the back of her head with one hand. "*Bite.*"

She did. Her fangs sank into his chest, right next to his breastbone. His teeth clenched as the pleasure doubled — tripled, and his cock swelled even more.

He let her drink, and her sex contracted around him in another orgasm. He loved those hot, little trembles around his cock — they made him even wilder.

He waited for them to stop, waited for her to pull her mouth from him, and when she did, he offered her a hard smile. "My way now."

Her cheeks were flushed, her eyes gleaming, and she just said, "Yes."

He withdrew from her. Lifted her up and whirled her to face one of the wooden posts on that bed. He caught her hands, but then stilled, utterly lost for a moment at the sight of his claws over her delicate fingers.

Stop. Don't hurt her. Pull back —

She looked over her shoulder at him. "I can see your fangs." But she didn't sound scared. "My…what sharp teeth you have, Julian." Her voice was breathless. Definitely not afraid. *Hungry.*

She wanted what he could give to her because a vampire's needs were so much darker than a human's. She didn't even realize how things could be between them.

She would. Soon enough.

He wrapped her hands around the post. "Hold tight." Then his gaze slid to her neck. It was bared to him. Her neck, the sweet curve of her shoulder. Just the spot he wanted.

His hand trailed over her back. His claws slid over her skin. He didn't cut her. Wouldn't. But…

He would bite.

He spread her legs and pulled her hips back against him. He drove into her from behind, and she arched against him, rocking her hips.

Julian's mouth pressed to the curve of her shoulder. His teeth raked her skin. He withdrew. He plunged deep. She moaned. She arched.

He bit.

A marking…because that was the way of his kind. His teeth punctured her, his two canines sinking deep.

"Julian!"

The cry wasn't one of pain. And the pleasure was just beginning. He lapped at her skin even as he drove into her. There was no control now. He took her deep and hard, getting lost in her as the beast and the man claimed the woman he'd always wanted for a mate.

Even if she didn't realize it.

She came again—came with a scream this time. He didn't stop. He couldn't. He thrust and withdrew, thrust and growled. His hands caught hers once more. He held her up against that post and he took her. Soon the pleasure was slamming into him and he roared his release. The climax was so intense his whole body shuddered. Pleasure filled every cell of his body. Pleasure that just went on and on, until he felt absolutely wrung out.

Distantly, he became aware of a dull thudding. His heartbeat—slowing down. Finally. Sweat coated his body and when he looked at his hands—his claws were disappearing. Soon he was just holding his hands over hers. Holding her.

She was so small next to him. Seemed so fragile.

Her head turned. She stared at him. And then she smiled.

Not so fragile now.

"I like it when you don't hold back."

He'd never hold back again.

She pressed her lips to his and the kiss was...oddly sweet. Tender. When he'd never been the tender type, except with her.

But then she turned her head away. She stiffened.

"OhmyGod..." Now Rose sounded horrified. "Tell me...*please tell me*...we didn't just leave that door open while we had sex."

His gaze shot to the door. To the open door. He'd left it open when he carried her to bed because he hadn't wanted her to feel like a prisoner.

And he couldn't help it. For the first time in longer than he could remember, Julian roared with laughter.

***

Simon put Keri on the boat. *Her* boat. Helpful human. He smiled at her and his index finger slid under her chin as he tipped her head up. "You remember what to do?"

She smiled back at him. "Yes."

"Good...good...do exactly what Simon says and you'll get to live another day."

Maybe.

Highly doubtful.

"I'll go to the island," she whispered.

Keri had turned out to be full of surprises. She owned her own boat, a nineteen-footer that she often took out on snorkeling trips. She knew the area well and…

She was going to be his perfect distraction.

He jumped off the vessel and untied the lines for her as she stood at the wheel. He looped the rope into his hand as he watched her. "You'll go to the island. You'll be my distraction."

Her hands curled around the wheel. "I'll find the lost girl for you."

Rose wasn't a girl and she wasn't exactly lost. But, yes, that was the general plan.

"And I'll kill anyone who gets in my way." Keri smiled at him as the boat's engine growled. She looked so innocent. So carefree.

She looked absolutely perfect. A human, heading right into a den of paranormals. Would they kill her on sight? Perhaps. That would be Keri's bad luck. But, if they didn't kill her, if they thought she was just an innocent human who'd gotten lost and wandered into their den…

Then maybe she'd have a chance to find his vampire.

Until he had Rose, his collection just wouldn't be complete.

CHAPTER SEVEN

She didn't like interrogations. She didn't like prison cells. And she didn't like the hard, predatory stare that Julian was giving to the human.

Rose was afraid that Francis might wet himself at any moment.

"This is...some kind of really big mistake." Francis paced in the cell. "I don't know what I did wrong, but I swear...I won't do it again."

Rayce choked out a laugh. He was watching from a few feet away. Her gaze jerked to him and when his stare met hers, she felt heat lance her cheeks.

The damn door was open! She knew the guy had heard every humiliating sound she'd made. Even if the door had been closed, though, he probably would have heard her. Stupid shifter hearing.

"Just let me go," Francis pleaded. Julian was in the cell with him. "I won't ever bother you again, man." He rushed toward Julian. "I swear, I—"

Julian's hand clamped around the guy's throat. Sighing, Julian lifted the kid up into the air, as if Francis weighed nothing. "I need to know about Simon."

Francis clawed at Julian's hand, but Julian didn't let him go. And it looked as if Francis's face was starting to turn purple.

Because he can't breathe.

"You're going to tell me everything you know about Simon. You're going to tell me about the Collector, and you're going to lead me to the missing paranormals."

Francis's mouth opened and closed — like a dying, desperate fish — but no sound emerged.

Rose surged forward and grabbed the bars on his cell. She didn't want to think too long or hard about why the Lord of the Dark had a prison installed on his island. A prison that you accessed through the guy's *house.* "He can't speak, Julian! You're killing him!"

Julian's head turned toward her. "There are two ways to do this."

"*Stop* killing him." That was way one for her.

He looked back at his prey. "The hard way...that's my way. A way that involves pain and loss of consciousness...at least a few times..."

"Julian..." Rose snapped.

He flashed a smile at her. "And then there's your way, love. The way you compel the truth from him, vamp style. If you're up to the challenge, come on in."

Step into my parlor...

But it wasn't a parlor. It was a cage. Something straight from her nightmares.

Julian dropped Francis. The human fell to the floor, gasping. "I...I don't...know...Simon!"

She saw Julian's claws emerge. He bent toward the fallen man. "Stop!" Rose yelled. Oh, damn, she was going to do this. She yanked open the cell door and stumbled inside. "I'll try, okay? Just...stop."

Julian's head lifted. He quirked a brow at her, as if to say...*Knew you'd come in.* And he had, of course. He'd played her.

"For a vamp, she's not very bloodthirsty, is she?" Rayce called out.

No, she wasn't. Rose exhaled on a slow breath. She rubbed her damp palms over her jeans. When she'd woken, fresh clothes had been waiting at the bottom of the bed for her. Jeans, t-shirt, shoes, even underwear. Everything had fit her perfectly. She had no idea where Julian had gotten the items, and she hadn't been in the mood to look a gift horse in the mouth. She'd just been happy to say good-bye to her blood-stained clothing.

"Are you working on that whole lack of bloodthirstiness?" The werewolf wanted to know. "Cause it's generally survival of the fittest, not the nicest, in our world."

She tossed him a glare. "How do you think you're helping here?"

He laughed. "You're right. Please, do your thing. I'd love to watch." He sauntered toward the cell.

"*Help me, lady.*" The desperate croak had her swinging her gaze back to Julian — and his prey. Francis's face was splotchy and red, and he looked terrified. "I don't know what's… happening…I just want to go home. Will you let me go home?"

She swallowed and knelt on the floor before him. Julian stood right behind Francis. "I am going to help you." She kept her voice low and easy. "I want you to just focus on me, okay? Look into my eyes."

Rayce snorted. "Jeez, that is just like one of those old black and white movies — "

"Shut the hell up, wolf," Julian snarled.

Rayce shut up.

Good. Great. "Look into my eyes," she said again, but she didn't feel like some monster from an old school movie. She felt more like a cobra, drawing in prey. Francis blinked, owlishly, and then stared into her eyes. She pushed forth her power — power that was currently running at high capacity thanks to the boost that she'd gotten from Julian's blood. She could feel the strength in her veins, surging forth. Rose knew she *could* compel a human, but that didn't mean she liked to do it.

Taking away someone's free will didn't exactly sit well with her.

"I want you to trust me, okay?" Her voice was soothing. She lifted her hand and touched his cheek. Julian tensed. *Uh, oh. Someone doesn't like me touching the human.* Too bad, he could just deal with it. "I won't hurt you. I'm just going to ask you a few questions, and you're going to answer me."

Easy enough. Simple enough.

Francis nodded. His mouth had gone slack and his eyes were unblinking as he gazed back at her.

A cobra's prey. No…a vamp's prey.

"Who strapped you into that vest on the *Pandora*? The vest that was wired with explosives?"

A croak came from his mouth. Just a croak. As if he were trying to speak, but couldn't.

She didn't look away from him. Looking away would lessen her control over his mind.

"Francis." She pushed more power forth. "Francis, tell me why you told us…'*Simon says*'…right before you activated that bomb?"

Sweat trickled down his face. Francis's body shuddered. "G-game…playing a game…"

Their near-deaths had been a game? Not likely. "Who told you to play the game?"

His breath shuddered out.

"*Tell* me the name of the person who ordered you to play the game."

Behind her, she heard a groan. "I thought this would work better," Rayce grumbled. "That it was supposed to be all wham-bam, you're under my control, and he instantly tells you everything." He sighed. "Julian, you may need to pull out the claws again."

Her shoulders stiffened. "No, he doesn't." Her gaze never left Francis's. "Give me the name of the person who ordered you to play the game."

"S-Simon…"

Right. Simon. Good. This was —

"S-Simon says…" A tear leaked from Francis's eye. "D-die…"

Not good. Not good at all.

Francis leapt to his feet. He ran past her, trying to get out of the cell, but Rayce was there and the werewolf just slammed the cell door shut before Francis could escape.

She thought Francis would stop once the door shut.

He didn't. He ran right into the closed door. He hit the bars hard enough to send his body shuddering back a few feet, and then, in the next blink, he was up and running for the bars again.

He hit them with his head. Again and again. Blood covered his face.

"Stop!" Rose yelled, but he didn't stop. So she and Julian lunged for him. They grabbed Francis at the same time. Already, one of his eyes had swollen shut from the impact. His lip was busted, his nose seemingly broken, and blood poured from a wound on his forehead.

"H-have to d-die…" Francis whispered. "Simon says…Simon says d-die and I-I do." He strained in their hold, and she had no doubt that, if he had broken free then, he would have just kept banging his head against those bars. He would have banged and banged until he killed himself.

Not exactly an easy way to go. Not exactly a way most folks would *choose.*

"He's still under someone else's compulsion." She had thought he was clear when they'd pulled him out of the water, but she'd been wrong. She could see it now. "The compulsion is buried deep, and when I push him, it comes forward to stop me. He's supposed to die before revealing the truth."

Rayce whistled. "That's one strong compulsion."

Julian dragged the guy across the room. "Bring in rope. We're going to need to tie this guy down so he doesn't hurt himself."

Rayce's footsteps hurried away.

Rose just stared at Francis, her heart hurting for him. He was helpless, a puppet who had no choice at all. A man who would die for something he didn't understand.

Life wasn't fair.

Rayce was back moments later. He and Julian tied Francis securely onto a chair, locking him down so that the guy couldn't move at all. When they were done, Julian stayed behind Francis, frowning down at him, and Rayce paced to Rose's side. "Didn't think compulsions were supposed to work like that."

"It's a strong compulsion," Julian said. "The only way to make one that cuts that deep is through blood or through some very powerful magic." A muscle flexed along his jaw. He looked damn unhappy as he added, "Just like the only way to break one that deep—"

"Is through blood," Rose finished. *Or magic.* And since she had no magic to speak of, her only hope was blood. She knew this. She might not like being a vamp but she'd tried to learn as much as she could about the undead life. The majority of that education had come from the Lord of the Dark himself. Right after her transformation, Luke had kept paying her pop-up visits. Until she'd told him to keep his ass away from her unless he could change her back.

He'd stayed away.

"So, you take his blood and you break the compulsion?" Rayce asked.

"Not exactly." She lifted her wrist to her mouth. Her fangs extended and she bit down, not deep, just enough to draw forth a few drops of blood. Then she closed the distance between her and the human. He leaned away from her and the scent of his fear thickened in the cell. "Hold his head steady, Julian."

Julian grabbed Francis's head and immediately stopped the guy's retreat, but then Julian's eyes blazed as he gritted out, "I do *not* like this."

It wasn't like the scene was a picnic in the park for her, either. "My blood will link him to me," she said quietly, so that Rayce would understand what was happening. Based on Julian's glare, it was obvious he already knew the score. "It will enable me to give him a new compulsion, one that cuts deeper than the other that's in place." A suicide compulsion—or at least, that was sure what it looked like to her. Someone had buried an order deep inside of Francis's mind. One that switched on like a protective mechanism. Only the order wasn't about protecting Francis's life—it was about protecting the identity of the person who'd originally compelled him.

She put her hand to his mouth. Her blood dripped past his lips. He tried to spit it back at her. "No, stop, that's gross—" Francis sputtered.

Julian shoved one hand over Francis's mouth, forcing the guy to keep the blood.

Rose leaned in close. "You *will* swallow that blood. You will take it."

Francis swallowed.

Her breath eased out. "Good. Now you will listen and you will obey me. You will *not* kill yourself. You want to live. You want to grow old and have a freaking fantastic life. The *last* thing you desire is to hurt yourself, in any way."

He wasn't blinking, just staring at her.

"Let him go, Julian," she said.

Julian backed away from the human.

"Who put you under the compulsion to ignite that bomb?" But she already knew. Dammit...

"Simon," he whispered. "Simon Lorne."

Her stomach twisted. "Tell me about when you met Simon."

"I...I was at a club. I'd had too much to drink...using my fake ID."

Jeez, he really *wasn't* even old enough to drink.

"I went out back. Was going to puke my guts out. When he—he just appeared." His words came fast, but they were low, a bit dazed sounding. "He grabbed me...asked if I wanted to play his game."

Only it wasn't really a game.

"What all did Simon tell you to do?" Rose asked him.

"He...he said to wait on the boat. He was bringing in a woman, someone he needed. Someone special. He needed me to have the boat ready to go for him."

Julian started to pace—no, more like prowl. A scary prowl because she was sure she'd just glimpsed the flash of his claws again.

"If he got to the boat with you, we were...we were going to meet the others. If he didn't come..." His words trailed away and he stared at her, his gaze still unblinking.

"What were you supposed to do if he didn't come?"

"I was supposed to destroy the boat. Destroy all ties to him. Because he has important work to finish."

Julian snarled. "I should have just killed that fucking bastard when I had the chance!" He whirled and pointed at her. "See? This is what happens when you try to do the *right* thing."

"I didn't know Simon was a killer!" An asshole, yes, she'd known that. But she hadn't realized he was the—the ring leader! Dammit. "I thought he was just some human following orders—someone like Francis!" She gestured to the bound man. "Simon *smelled* human. He acted human, and he sure was screaming like a terrified human when he was trapped in that SUV."

Julian frowned. "Yes, he was." Now he seemed puzzled. "I thought he was human, too."

Rayce cleared his throat. "Okay, so I'll point out the obvious. Julian, you're a shifter. That means you have the best sense of smell on the planet."

"Sh-shifter…?" Francis croaked. "Shifters…vampires…"

They all ignored him. Rayce noted, "If you thought the guy smelled human, then odds are high that he *is* human. Not like we have a monopoly on evil, you know. Sometimes, humans can be worse than we are." His voice roughened. "I've sure seen that shit first-hand."

So a human was hunting her? No, that didn't fit. "A human couldn't work a compulsion."

"Not without help," Julian agreed. "The magical kind. So we have to figure out just where he's getting that help."

She eyed Francis. "You said he was going to take me to the others." Rose crossed her arms over her body. "If he has other paranormals, then he could be using their powers some way. Maybe that's why he's after us all." She leaned in close to Francis. "Where were you going to meet the others? Where are they?"

"I-I don't know."

"But you said you were going to meet the others—"

"Francis here was just an insurance policy. Someone to make sure that whatever this Simon had left on his boat—that it didn't make it into the wrong hands," Rayce cut in. "I'm guessing the destination was plugged into the GPS or some shit like that. So your mysterious buddy Simon could have been heading out to one of the islands that dot the coast. Or he could have been going back to the mainland. He wanted the boat for a fast exit, and he wanted expendable Francis there in case something went wrong with his plan."

Hell. "Do you remember *anything* that might help us?" Rose asked Francis.

His brows beetled down. "He…he said we were going where no one would find us. Only the gators could see him."

Gators?

"My money's on the mainland," Rayce said. "Maybe the Everglades? Stretches for freaking miles and miles. That would be the perfect place to hide."

"Is there anything else?" Rose asked Francis. "Anything else that can help me?"

Francis just stared at her. "What are you?" Then his gaze flew to Julian and Rayce. "What are you *all?*" His terror was back.

But she knew how to handle that fear. She put her hand under his chin and turned his battered face back toward her. "You never met us. You were never on this island. You're going to sleep, and when you wake up, you'll be back in Key West. You partied too much and you can't remember anything...now all you want to do is go home and forget this trip."

"Forget this trip," he whispered.

"Right. Forget it and live a normal life." *Be one of the lucky ones.* "Now get your ass to sleep."

His eyes sagged closed.

She exhaled on a rough sigh and stepped away from him. Her gaze darted to Julian and Rayce. "See? No need to hurt the guy. He told us plenty." Rose pushed back her shoulders. "And there's no need to *kill* him, either. He won't remember any of us or this place, and he can just be taken back to Key West and left there."

"Uh, huh..." Julian didn't look convinced. "What happens if Simon appears and decides to attack him? What then?"

"Well, we just have to find Simon first." She inclined her head toward Rayce. "You can make sure Francis is safe until he can leave the Keys, and Julian and I—we'll find Simon."

Julian growled.

Rose put her hands on her hips. "What? You're going to tell me that if we head back to the wreck scene you *won't* be able to follow his scent?

Because I'm not buying it." She turned on her
heel and marched for the cell door — one that had
been left open by Rayce when he came charging
in with the rope. Her priority was getting out of
that cell. Only…when she started walking, Rose
found she couldn't stop. She rushed through the
thin security tunnel she'd entered earlier, feeling
almost claustrophobic now that she'd done her
part.

She hurried through the house and grabbed
for the front door. She wrenched it open, and
sunshine poured down on her. Fresh air blew
against her face and the scent of the ocean teased
her nose. Rose hurried outside, so glad to be free.
Out of the cell. In the open. She was —

"Did he say something to you?" Julian's low
voice came from behind her. "When Simon had
you in the SUV with him, did he say something
you haven't told me?"

Her hand lifted to her neck. Her wrist wasn't
bleeding any longer. She'd healed, the way
vamps could heal so quickly. She remembered
Simon jabbing the needle into her neck. The cold
rush as the drug had gone through her veins. "He
told me I was the vampire he'd been looking for."

"For his collection."

That just creeped her out. Who collected
people? Or paranormals?

She looked toward the ocean. She could see a
boat in the distance. For a moment, she wished

that she could be on that boat, sailing far away. "He said…he said the guys who tried to jump us in the alley were his back-up." What had happened to them? Were they somewhere nursing wounds? Were they already back with Simon?

"Anything else?"

"No." Rose shook her head. Her hand fell back to her side. "He shoved the needle into me, and I pretty much don't remember anything else until I woke up and saw you." She looked back at him. "You got me out of the wreck, didn't you?"

His head inclined.

"Did I tell you thank you?" Now her voice had gone soft.

"Nothing to thank me for."

Her lips twisted. "Just the little matter of saving my life. I could smell the gasoline. I saw the flames when the vehicle ignited. If you hadn't come along, Simon and I both would have died."

Julian came toward her with his slow, gliding steps. The back of his hand rose and slid down her cheek. It was a familiar caress. "And the world would have gone fucking dark without you."

He did that sometimes—just said things that made it hard for her to breathe. He made her want things she couldn't have. Because…

Deep down, so very deep, the truth was that she feared Julian. She wanted him, needed him, but feared him nonetheless. He'd taken her choice away from her before. How could she trust that he wouldn't do it again?

And what about the kills he'd made? The story of him being Luke's assassin? Was it true?

"It's because I'm a vampire, isn't it?" She was actually turning her head toward his touch, as if hungry for it. "I carry a darkness now and that darkness—it likes you."

His jaw clenched. "Is that what you think is happening between us?"

"I don't know what's happening." A pause, then she said, "I know you scare me."

He flinched.

"When I first met you, I wasn't afraid. I only felt safe with you. So totally safe. It was strange. I thought I could trust you completely. Something just clicked for me when I saw you."

His gaze raked her face. "Then you found out the truth."

"I found out the truth and I lost my life…all in the same night." The sun was warm on her face and she was so glad that particular tale was fake—vampires could stay in the sunlight. It made her weaker, yes, but right then, she didn't care. She needed to be outside, just as she needed to get these words out. "I woke up and everything was different. When I ran outside, I could hear too much, I could see things too brightly. My head felt as if it were going to explode, and I was so *hungry*. I drank your blood in the road, and I was horrified."

"Rose—"

She held up her hand, as if warding him off. "Let me finish. Please." Because they needed to talk. "I took your blood, and I liked it."

"There's nothing wrong with that. *You're a vampire.*"

He didn't get it. "It was wrong for me. I ran because I couldn't stand what I'd done."

His hands had clenched at his sides.

"For days, I was starving, and I couldn't take blood from anyone else. It made me sick to think of drinking it. I had nearly starved myself to death when Luke showed up."

His eyes turned to glittering slits.

"He made me drink from humans. But I vomited the blood up, again and again." She remembered vomiting on Luke.

He hadn't been amused.

But then, she hadn't been amused, either.

"I begged Luke to change me back during those first terrible weeks. Again and again, I begged him."

Shock flashed on Julian's face. "He didn't— he never said—"

"I didn't want to kill anyone else. I thought I couldn't drink without murdering a human. I didn't want that." Her lips pressed together. "Luke...he was the one who had to go with me on my first few hunts. He was the one that had to stand in the shadows and make sure I didn't go too far. He'd stop me before I killed. He made sure that I — I learned to control myself."

But she'd still hated every moment of her new hell.

"He was there. A man I didn't know. A man I hated." She sucked in a deep breath as she took a few steps back. "Where were you?" The question burst from her. It was a question that had haunted her for a very long time. *I needed you. You weren't there. Where were you?*

A mask settled over his face. Hard. Unreadable. "You didn't want me close. You told me to stay the hell away from you."

"I was *terrified.* I was out of my mind." And yes, she had said that. Right after she'd pleaded with him to change her back. Her heart lurched in her chest. "When I first woke up in that bed, you were barely talking. You had blood all over you — "

"Because I'd fucking killed the men who shot you." He surged toward her. Towered over her. "Did you really think I'd let them get away with what they'd done? They were there for me. *My* enemies. They used their fucking heat sensors to see that we were near the front door, and they shot through it, through *you* in order to hit me." His hand pressed to her chest, right over her heart. "The bullets had *your* blood on them when they sank into me. I heard you cry out. I *felt* you dying. There was no way I was going to let those cowards get away with what they'd done. I summoned Luke. I made a deal to save you. And then I cut their fucking heads from their bodies."

She flinched.

"*That* is who I am. I am retribution. I am punishment. Luke had used me before and after that night, he used me plenty more. When paranormals crossed the line, when they needed to be put down because all they were doing was bringing torment to the humans around them, my job was to stop the monsters. I'm a killer, a very good one, and I promised Luke I'd kill as many paranormals as he wanted, provided he did one thing for me. Just one." His breath heaved out. "He let you live. That he brought you *back*."

Her mouth had gone dry. Her heart drummed too fast in her chest. "B-back?" That was a thought that chilled her. She'd somehow always thought that she'd been on the verge of dying, and that Luke had transformed her right before her human self crossed that last, thin line. She hadn't realized that she'd been...gone. Or maybe, maybe that was just what she had *wanted* to believe.

But just where had she gone to? Rose shivered.

"You died. I watched it happen. I saw the life leave your eyes as I held you in my arms." He exhaled. His hands fell to his sides and clenched into fists. "And greedy bastard that I am, I wasn't going to let things end that way. I brought you back, I made Luke find a way, and I turned you into a monster."

Back. Where had I been?

Heaven?

Hell?

She had no memory of either place. She just remembered the pain of the bullets as they tore into her. She remembered Julian's wild roar. She remembered not being able to feel his hands on her skin.

Then…

She'd been in the bed. Waking up to fear.

Rose licked her lips. "I didn't even know monsters existed until that night."

"And then you found out I was one of the baddest of them all." He gave a grim laugh. "I saw how you looked at me when you opened your eyes. You were in that bed, blood still on your skin, and you stared at me as if I were the one who'd fired those bullets into you."

It was her turn to flinch because she knew he spoke the truth.

"But then, I guess I kind of was…right? You were hit, because of me. You died, because of me. So it only seemed fair that I find a way to make you live again. And, no, I didn't fucking ask if that was what you wanted. There wasn't time to ask. *You were gone.* I didn't stop to think that you wouldn't want to become someone like me. I wasn't thinking at all. For a time there, I...went a little mad."

Once more, she looked back toward the water. Sometimes, it was too hard to look into his eyes. "Where did you go, after I woke up?" Her lips twisted in a humorless smile. "After I told you to stay the hell away from me."

"I had a debt to pay. I hunted. I killed."

"For Luke."

"For you."

No, no, she didn't want to think of anyone dying for her. "They were...what?" Now she gave a brittle laugh. "The bad paranormals? Are you some kind of paranormal Dexter, eliminating the threats so that everyone else can be safe?"

"I don't fucking know Dexter."

Her gaze shot back to him.

"I only know Luke doesn't put anyone in my path unless there is no other option. Do I kill the worst scum out there? Yes. I take out the vampires who drain innocent kids. I stop the werewolves who tear teenage girls limb from limb. Luke rules the dark. That means he is judge and jury, and I'm his executioner."

She just—

He reached for her. His claws were out.

She stumbled back. "I need...I need some time alone, okay?"

He stared at his hands. At his razor sharp claws "Do you still see the blood there?"

"Julian..."

"Because I do. The only time I couldn't see it...it was during that brief time when I was with you. When you made me feel like I was someone else." His hands hung between them. His claws slowly retracted. "You want to know why I didn't tell you the truth sooner? It was because humans aren't supposed to know. They can't handle the real shit that's around them. That's the—"

"Paranormal law. Yes, I know it." *Now.*

"That wasn't the only reason, though. I break plenty of laws." His hands lowered back to his sides. A faint smile tilted the corners of his lips. If anything, that smile made him appear more sinister. "I liked pretending to be normal. It was a fantasy, but it was a damn fine one. Imagining what it would be like, to have a human life. To have a woman like you. To go out on dates and make love and do everything else a normal man does."

But in the end, the fantasy had ended. He hadn't become human. She'd become the vampire.

And now she was hunted. She always seemed to be. *Go after the weak.* That was the motto in the paranormal world. It appeared everyone could sense just how weak she was. A vamp who hated drinking blood. A vamp who felt guilty when she used compulsions. A vamp who had to literally psych herself up so that she could hunt.

I am evil. That was her hunting mantra.

It was utter bullshit.

"The island is safe for you. I had Marcos take the other paranormals away before dawn. So it's just me, you and Rayce." His lips tightened. "And the human, for now."

The waves crashed against the shore and the sound was oddly soothing to her.

"So if you want to go off on your own for a while, do it. Get your space. Run free. I needed to run last night. Only seems fair that you get the same chance now. Go. I'll be here when you come back."

His words sounded like a promise.

She started walking toward the beach. Rose wouldn't let herself look back at him.

CHAPTER EIGHT

An angel wasn't supposed to be in hell.

Lila stared at her wings. A pale imitation of what they'd once been. She'd already lost so many feathers, and the others didn't shine any longer. They were darker.

Weaker.

Just as she was weak.

"Hey, angel!" Another female voice called out to her. Her head turned, and she saw the muse frowning at her.

She didn't know the muse's name, just what she was. A muse inspired humans. Sent them soaring to incredible heights...because she obsessed them. Her power was dark. She focused the mortals on their task to the extent that they lost focus on everything else.

Her magic was deadly.

And she was supposed to be an angel's enemy.

"Don't cry, angel," the muse said, her voice soft. "We're going to get out of here." She moved closer to the bars of her own cell and Lila saw the glint of the woman's blonde hair.

Was she crying? Lila lifted a hand and touched her cheek. She was surprised by the wetness she felt there. Angels weren't supposed to cry.

Angels weren't supposed to feel.

So many things we aren't "supposed to" do.

"Don't lie to her." It was the other woman's voice...the witch. Another being that Lila was supposed to stay far away from because a witch was a dark paranormal. "Don't give her false hope. We're all dying in this hell." She came toward the bars of her cell. Her beautiful face showed sympathy as she looked at Lila. "Better go ahead and accept it now." Her hands lifted. She had such gorgeous coffee cream skin. When Lila had first met the witch, the other woman had seemed to glow with power. Her whole body had seemed to shine with an inner light. But that light had been fading. Slowly, day by day.

"I'm not lying," the muse shot back, sounding annoyed. "I'm trying to *inspire.* It's kind of my thing, you know."

The witch laughed.

The witch and the muse. She thought they might be friends, of a sort.

"Your thing is to screw with the minds of mortals," the witch threw back. "Don't even try that shit with us."

Maybe they weren't friends.

Lila cleared her throat. "Our captor...he's human. Why doesn't your 'thing' work on him?"

There was silence, and she thought the muse wouldn't answer her. She shouldn't have spoken. They knew just how different from them she truly was. They were dark paranormals, bound to Luke Thorne, while she was tied to his twin brother, the Lord of the Light.

Tied to Leo.

Or...to the "dick" as the muse had called him.

Though she didn't think he was a dick. Leo was her friend. When she'd first been taken, Lila had been so sure that Leo would come find her. But the days had slipped by.

He hadn't appeared.

"I can't do my 'thing' on him," the muse muttered, "because he's already obsessed enough. Why do you think we're all here?"

"I have no idea." No, that wasn't true. He'd been taking her power away, one feather at a time. "I thought he wanted our magic."

"Oh, he does." The witch laughed. "But he wants it because he has a purpose. A plan."

"What plan?"

"This is just going to make her cry more," the muse warned. She seemed to be scolding the witch.

The witch backed away from her bars.

"Ignore her," the muse ordered. She flashed Lila a smile.

She's beautiful, too. All muses were supposed to be beautiful. It was part of their charm. Leo had said creatures like the muse were beautiful on the outside, but rotten on the inside.

The muse didn't seem rotten, though.

"The witch is mad," her voice carried easily to Lila, "because the jerkoff who took us locked down her magic. She's too weak to crack a spell and get our sorry asses out of this place."

The witch began cursing. Very inventive curses.

The muse laughed.

"I need a fourth," the witch muttered. "Air, fire, earth, and wind. If I could get all that, we'd be in business."

"I'm guessing the angel counts as air..." The muse tapped her foot. "What are you, witch? Fire?"

"No, that's you. You burn right through a man's soul, leaving only obsession in your wake."

The muse glanced down. "You say it like I have a choice."

Lila frowned.

"I'm wind," the witch said. "My power blows down my enemies. When I'm not fucking *imprisoned* by a freak."

Lila licked her lips. "What...what kind of being would be your earth?"

The muse replied, "Probably someone who's been dead. Earth to earth, ashes to ashes and all that jazz."

Nervously, Lila slipped back a step. "And what happens if we *do* get a fourth?"

The witch laughed. "I make hell come to town."

That didn't sound good.

"Want to know the other option, sweet angel?" The witch's voice had dropped. "The other option is that the jerkoff kills us all. Because he is *never* going to let us go. He does have a plan, and for that plan to work, he's going to destroy us."

She stopped retreating. Her wings curled closer to her body.

"When the time comes..." the witch stared at her with dark eyes. "Will you fight with us?"

Angels weren't supposed to fight. Her chin lifted. "Yes."

CHAPTER NINE

"That little one-on-one didn't go so well, did it?" Rayce murmured.

Julian had just marched back into the main house. He paused in the doorway, glaring at the wolf who was his semi-friend.

"I ask because well…you came back in without the girl."

"She's not a girl. She's a woman."

"Right. Yes, absolutely. I mean you came back in without the sexy vampire who — " His words broke off because Julian had lunged forward and grabbed the guy by the throat. Julian shoved Rayce against the nearest wall. Rayce's flailing hands hit a table and a vase crashed.

Luke would be pissed. So what?

"Watch what you say about her." He eased his hold, just enough for Rayce to speak.

"What's wrong with what I said? The woman is gorgeous! She's sexy as all hell. I've always had a thing for women with bite and — "

He tightened his hand on Rayce's throat. "Why the hell do you push me?" Disgusted, he let the guy go. "Bugger off, mate."

Rayce cleared his throat. Once. Twice. And he didn't bugger off. "As I was saying…" He flashed a smile — one that showed his own lengthening canines. "I've always had a thing for women with bite and apparently, so do you."

Julian nailed him with a right hook.

Rayce grunted and took a step back. "What the ever-loving hell? Dude, get control of your jealousy. Seriously." He rubbed his jaw. "In a minute, I'll stop being nice and I'll fight back."

"That hit wasn't from jealousy." His eyes raked the werewolf. "It was because you freaking locked her up. She *hates* being locked up. Rose had tears on her cheeks." His hand lifted. He should hit the jerk again.

But Rayce's eyes had widened in shock. "What? Shit, look, I thought I was *helping*. I'm a helper. That's what I do."

Julian snorted. "Don't feed me that tosh."

"Tosh?" Rayce blinked. "You're throwing out your British shit again—"

"Crap," Julian gritted out. "Don't feed me your bull." Rayce was a rogue wolf. He might put up a veneer of humor and charm, but the guy was a ravenous killer. He had no pack, so that made him even more dangerous. He wasn't an alpha — he was one step *above* that power level. So all the other wolves in the world were terrified of him. And when you feared something, what did you do?

You avoided it. You ran from it.

Just like Rose was running from him.

His shoulders fell.

"Are you really going to take her back to the mainland?" Rayce wanted to know. "I mean, is that a good idea? She can stay here. You know that. She can stay here and —"

"Be locked up?" So she could hate him even more? Julian shook his head. "I said I'd stay by her side every minute. That was the deal I made, and I've already slipped on that deal too much as it is." Because when they'd first returned to the island, he'd shifted and left her alone. It had only been the distance of a few acres, and that still counted as close, didn't it? "I don't know how much he'll allow for the deal."

As soon as the words were out of his mouth, Julian knew he'd made a mistake.

"Deal?" Rayce repeated as he tilted his head. "You made another deal with Luke? Didn't you learn from last time?"

He looked away. "I didn't say the deal was with Luke."

"Yes, but why would you make a deal with anyone else? You're a paranormal powerhouse, just like me." Rayce didn't say the words as if he were bragging. More like just stating a fact. And, yes, it was a fact. "There's no one you need to barter with, no one who can help you except…" His words trailed away and horror — real, honest-to-goodness horror filled his eyes. And Rayce wasn't the type to easily be horrified. "Tell me you didn't."

"I didn't." He turned away and headed for his room. The room he'd wrecked with Rose. Why had she let him touch her if she was still afraid?

Her voice echoed through his mind. *It's because I'm a vampire, isn't it? I carry a darkness now and that darkness — it likes you.* Part of what she'd said was true. Her desires were darker now that she was a vamp. His desires had always been dark. Nearly insatiable.

But when he was with her…

"You British asshole, stop!"

Julian frowned and glanced back.

Rayce's cheeks were flushed. "You lied to me."

Why was that an issue? "You lie to me all the time."

"No, no, you made a deal." Rayce pointed a finger at him. "And you did it with the good one, didn't you?"

Tread carefully. "You'll have to be more specific."

Rayce's cheeks flushed even redder. "You made a deal with Luke's freaking twin! You made a deal with Leo!" He marched forward, glaring the whole way as Julian turned to fully face him. "He's the only one who can match Luke's power. And since Luke has gone all AWOL on us with his new lady, Leo *would* be the only one around for you to deal with."

Luke Thorne was the Lord of the Dark — the ruler of every dark paranormal to walk the earth. And his twin brother Leo…Leo led the so-called light paranormals. The ones who were supposed to be good for humanity.

Only things weren't really black and white in the world, and, according to every legend that Julian had ever heard, an old prophecy had foretold that one day, the twins would battle to the death.

Then hell would truly reign.

"You can't trust Leo. Tell me you realize this."

"Don't worry about it."

A growl broke from Rayce. "I do worry about it. What do you think he'll do? Help your lady? Give her back a human life? Cause that can't happen. There *is* no going back. She died. If she stops being a vamp, she'll turn into a corpse."

Julian's muscles clenched.

"What did you offer him?" Now worry edged Rayce's voice. "I mean, that guy isn't going to bargain easily. He's like Luke that way."

The twins were alike in many ways. That was the problem.

"Tell me what you did. Tell me, man, so I can help you."

Julian raked a hand over his face. "I agreed to find someone for him."

Rayce's eyes widened. "Leo is freaking all-knowing—"

"No, he's not. He just likes to act that way."

"—and you mean to tell me he's lost one of *his* paranormals and can't find the guy?"

"Not a guy. It's a woman." This was the tricky part. "An angel."

Rayce rocked back a step. "Fucking hell."

"The Collector has her—that same SOB who thinks he is going to get his hands on Rose. Leo is the one who told me about him. He warned me that the Collector was coming after Rose and that's how I was able to get to her and save her sweet ass."

Rayce's brows climbed. "How did Leo know the guy was targeting her?"

"His angel managed to send him a message. She got to one of the Collector's guards. You know how angels have a way of turning humans to their sides…Well, she pulled at a guard, found his soft spot, and got a message to Leo. She warned him who the next target would be—"

"Because her kind always wants to save the world," Rayce muttered.

Yes, they did. That was kind of their thing. "And the guard was supposed to give Leo the angel's location, too. But the guy barely got out the warning about Rose before he died. Leo said the fellow's heart burned from *inside* his body."

Rayce blinked. Then he blinked again. "That's a...new one."

Yes, it was.

"Witchcraft?" Rayce wondered. "Maybe one seriously powerful spell?"

"I don't know, but I'm hoping to find out. Leo said magic is blocking him from finding the angel. He wants her back, badly. Badly enough to make a deal with me. I get her, and he will give me what I want."

"We both know what you want."

Julian forced his back teeth to unclench. "If I don't save the angel, there's no deal. I have to find her, so that means I have to track the Collector to his fucking hole. I'll get all the paranormals he has imprisoned there, and then I'll do what I do best."

They both knew exactly what that was.
Kill.

"I'll have your back." Rayce's voice was quiet. "You know I stand with you."

"Thanks." He turned away once more. He'd only taken a few steps when...

"Thought I heard something...interesting this morning. Some unusual noise coming from your side of the house."

Oh, the wanker had better *not* say anything about Rose—

He tossed a glare back, his muscles tensing.

But there was no mockery on Rayce's face. For once, Rayce appeared very, very serious. "It sounded like you were laughing."

Julian's lips pressed together.

"It sounded like you were happy."

Again, he didn't speak. He headed down the hallway.

But he clearly heard Rayce's words as they followed him. "If someone made me happy like that, I'd fucking fight with every breath to keep her with me."

That was exactly what Julian planned to do.

***

A boat was coming toward the shore.

Rose stood on the beach. She'd taken off her shoes and the water tickled her toes. Her gaze was on the boat. It bobbed in the water, but kept coming closer and closer. She couldn't help but wonder, who would be brave enough—or dumb enough—to visit the Lord of the Dark's island?

It was not like she *wanted* to be there, and, soon enough, she'd be hauling ass back to the mainland.

But who was coming to visit the island right then? She lifted a hand, trying to shield her eyes from the sun. She'd been outside too long, she knew it. Her body felt leaden as exhaustion pulled at her. That was always the way it felt with too much sun exposure. It was her body's way of protesting. A vamp protest.

The boat bumped along, drawing ever closer to the island. Fear snaked down her spine and she started to edge back. Would the Collector come out there?

There was no magical force field or anything like that in place to stop folks from getting to the island. And that boat — it was almost there. It was heading straight for the dock. She spun around.

And nearly slammed into Julian's chest.

"Gah!" She gave a mini-scream. "Stop doing that! Stop sneaking up on me, shifter-style."

He frowned at her. "You're a vamp. You have enhanced hearing."

"And you move too quietly for me to hear you!" She had grabbed hold of his arms to steady herself. It took an effort, but she made her hands let him go. "Someone's coming."

"I know. I *heard* them when I was up at the house."

Her eyes narrowed. That had been a dig at her. "We don't all have shifter ears," she mumbled.

He caught her wrist with his gentle hold. "I want you to stay at the house while I take care of the visitor."

"Is 'take care' just another way of saying 'kill'?"

He didn't answer. So, yes, that silence *was* an answer.

"Julian, I think this is a bad idea." Death wasn't always the answer. It wasn't even always close to the answer. "Let's just see—"

Smoke. Her nose twitched and she looked back at the boat to see black tendrils of smoke drifting from the rear of the vessel. "The motor's on fire."

Then she saw a figure—a woman in shorts with long, blonde hair. The woman was waving frantically from the boat and calling for—

"*Help!*" The woman's shout reached Rose as a whisper and she took a step forward.

"No." Julian pushed her back. "Absolutely not. I *get* that you're out to rescue the world and all, but this scene has trap written all over it."

"It has desperate woman written all over it!"

"Go back to the house. Stay inside. If she's just some lost tourist, I'll send her on her way. Marcos can tow her vessel back to Key West. If she's not…then I'll make sure she doesn't cause any other trouble."

"We're supposed to stay together. You said —"

"For the moment, I want you to stay in the house. I'll just take a quick trip out there with Marcos and see what's happening. Generally, we try not to arouse suspicions with humans. If she *is* just human, we'll make her understand this is private property."

But he was still ditching her. "Promise you won't go to Key West without me. If this is some kind of trick and you're just lying to me so that you can sail away and leave me trapped here —"

His hold tightened on her wrist. "I'm not lying to you. Stay inside until I assess the threat, then we'll go, *together,* back to Key West."

Okay. Good. She could deal with that.

"Take her in, Rayce."

She'd actually known the wolf was behind her. Rose had caught his scent just a moment before. Since she couldn't hear the shifters approach, Rose was trying to focus on recognizing their scents to warn her of their presence.

She turned from Julian and made her way toward the wolf.

"I don't like this," she muttered to Rayce.

"You and me both," he rasped right back.

***

"Ahoy!" Marcos Minos called as he drew the *Devil's Prize* closer to the other boat.

"Oh, thank God!" The woman with the long hair gave Marcos and Julian a brilliant smile. "My motor overheated, and I thought I'd have to call a tow from Key West, and then, you know, it could be *hours* before they got out here."

The *Devil's Prize* was just a few feet away from her vessel.

"Please tell me that one of you knows a lot about motors," she pleaded, her smile winking again.

Marcos looked at Julian.

Julian held his gaze a moment, communicating that Marcos was not to move, not yet, then he glanced back at the woman. "You're out here alone?"

"Yes, I am—wait, I'm not supposed to say that, am I?" She gave a nervous laugh. "I mean, you're always supposed to say that you have a buddy with you for safety if strangers ask..."

No one else was on the boat. He didn't hear anyone else. Didn't smell anyone else.

"But you two are my heroes, right?" she continued. Her hands ducked behind the railing. "You're not going to hurt me?"

"We don't have any plans to hurt you," Marcos called.

It was *looking* as if they didn't.

"That's good." Her smile came back, but her hands stayed down. "What happened to the woman on the beach? Where did she go?"

Julian tensed.

"I really need to find her..." And the woman lifted her hands. She had a gun gripped in one. Without another word, she fired — first at Julian, and the blast hit him in the chest. *Fucking hell.* The pain slammed hard into him, burning and he stumbled back. He fell onto the deck of the *Devil's Prize* even as he saw her swing the gun toward Marcos.

Marcos was human. A shot could kill him.

And Marcos...

He's my friend.

Roaring, Julian leapt up.

"I'm really sorry about this," the woman was saying. "But I don't have a choice. I have to distract, you see. Death has to come."

The bullet fired. But it didn't hit Marcos because Julian was in front of him. The bullet thudded into Julian's side and that was when he realized that it wasn't just a regular round.

He could feel the drug spreading through his system. Thickening. Numbing him. He sagged to his knees.

She fired again. This time, she hit Marcos.

"I have to find the woman from the beach," she said. "Where did she go?" She tucked the gun into her waistband and jumped into the water. Julian struggled to keep his eyes open. She'd smelled human. She'd seemed innocent.

He should have known fucking better. He was softening because of Rose. Becoming weak. That couldn't be allowed.

The woman pulled herself onto the *Devil's Prize*. Water dripped down her body as she came toward him. She grabbed his head, tipping it back and he was just fucking helpless. Couldn't even move at all.

She shoved the gun under his chin. "It got wet, so it might not fire…"

He stared at her. That was all he could do.

"How many guards are on the island? Where's the girl?"

Even if he could have talked, he wouldn't have said a word.

"Fine then." She sighed. And she shot him again. Despite being soaking wet, the gun worked and the tranq bullet flew up through his chin.

CHAPTER TEN

Rayce stiffened just as they reached the front door of the house. "Gunfire."

Yes, she'd heard it, too. And Rose had already whirled and started running back down that path, but then Rayce grabbed her, jerking her to a stand-still.

"No! Dammit, this could be a trap!"

Everything could be a trap these days. "Julian…"

"Is a big fucking shifter who can take care of himself. He's got killer claws and if I let you run into danger, he'll use those claws on *me*." Rayce's face was grim. "Get inside the house. I'll set the security and you'll be safe in there."

Why did people persist in treating her like a helpless human? She wasn't. Far from it. "We are wasting time." Then, using her vamp strength, she shoved him away from her. "If Julian needs me, I'm there."

She didn't wait for another argument. She turned and rushed down the path. She'd gone only a few frantic feet when she heard the cry.

"Help me!" A woman's voice, drifting on the wind. *"Help…"*

She and Rayce didn't say another word. They ran toward that call and then they saw her. A woman with long hair, soaking wet, stumbling up the path. Her hands were at her sides, her body weaving.

"Please…" The woman fell to her knees. *"Help me."*

"Human," Rayce said.

A human right in front of them and Julian nowhere to be seen.

Rose locked her legs and stared at the woman with fury growing in her. "What did you do?"

The woman's head had fallen forward. Her body had curled in on itself, but at Rose's words, her head tipped back. She smiled. "Found you." Glee was in her voice. Satisfaction. And then she yanked her hand up. She'd grabbed a weapon from beneath her shirt, one she'd hidden. She pointed it at Rose and pulled the trigger.

But Rose leapt to the side. The bullet missed her even as Rayce gave a guttural cry and sprang forward. He bounded toward the woman and she fired at him. Shooting once, twice.

One bullet hit him in the shoulder. He didn't stop. He grabbed her, his hands going right for the woman's throat. The gun dropped from her hand and clattered to the ground.

His hands tightened around her neck.

He was going to kill her.

Rose grabbed him. "She could be under compulsion! Just like Francis! Don't kill her, not yet, don't—"

He hesitated. Then he blinked and his gaze seemed to turn hazy.

"It's in you now," the woman whispered.

Rayce staggered.

"Special. He said no one could resist it. Too strong..."

Rose grabbed for Rayce when his body slumped forward.

"*Found you, found you,*" the woman sang.

She had grabbed her gun again. She aimed it at Rose. "He said you wouldn't want to hurt a human. He said that would make things so much easier. Rules are in place, and you're not supposed to cross the line. You're not supposed to hurt any human." Her smile stretched. "You're not supposed to—"

Wind blew against them. Fierce, hot, battering. Only that wind wasn't coming from the ocean. It was coming from above them. In a flash, a man landed right behind the human woman. He was tall, dark, with eyes that seemed to blaze with power. And he had fucking wings coming out of his back.

Giant, dark wings. Not soft, instead, they appeared razor sharp—scaled? *Dragon wings.* The wings just seemed to shoot right through the back of the t-shirt that he wore.

The human whirled toward him but he yanked the gun right from her and crushed it in his grip. "Don't quote my own rules back to me," he snarled. "That shit just makes me angry."

Then he touched the woman. Just put his hand to her forehead. She gasped and then her body collapsed as she literally fell into an unconscious heap at his feet.

Rose still had her grip on Rayce. She lowered him slowly to the ground but never took her eyes off the man before her. A man that she recognized. After all, it was pretty hard to forget the Lord of the Dark. "Luke," she whispered. She should have known that Luke Thorne would be showing up sooner or later. After all, this was his island.

And she was one of his creatures.

But the dark-haired man shook his head. "Wrong twin." His wings vanished, gone in a blink as if they'd never been there. Then he gave her a hard smile. "I'm the other one. Leo."

She scrambled back. Luke—she could deal with Luke. She might fear him, but he'd saved her life, or, given her a new one or something before. She knew he wouldn't hurt her. He'd actually popped into her life to help her in his weird way a few times. But this guy...

He was an exact copy of Luke in looks. Every detail was the same. The same square jaw, the same thick, dark hair. The same gleaming, too-knowing eyes. But their physical appearance was where the similarities ended. This guy wasn't tied to the dark paranormals. The stories said he had no love for shifters, vampires, or demons. The stories said he wanted them all *gone.*

He cared about the humans. He watched over them. He guarded the "good" paranormals — the angels, the Fates, the mermaids.

He wasn't there to protect her.

He wasn't there to help her.

So that meant...

She bared her fangs at him, ready to attack if he so much as took a step her way.

He raised one brow. "Easy vamp. I might be pissed as all hell that you even exist..."

Her whole body went tight. *Bastard.*

"But I'm not here to hurt you." A muscle jerked along his jaw. "And isn't there supposed to be a certain panther at your side? I specifically told that cat to keep you with him, all the damn time."

Wait, wait...*he'd* told Julian to stay with her?

Leo crossed his arms over his chest. "If he isn't going to keep up his end of things, then the deal is off."

What deal?

But…

She looked down at Rayce. He was out cold, but when she touched his neck, she felt his pulse beating.

"A tranq gun," Leo offered, as if she hadn't already figured that out. "I've got to say, the Collector is certainly playing a smart game. He's created a tranq more powerful than any I've seen before. It worked amazingly fast. I thought the werewolf would be able to take a couple of hits before he went down." He made a humming sound. "Wonder if that's the case with all shifters or if the werewolves just have a particular weakness to this new brew?"

Her head jerked back as she glared up at him. "Why? Are you thinking you might use it against them?"

He shrugged. *Shrugged.* And he was supposed to be the good one. "Get *away* from me," she barked at him.

Leo's eyes widened. "I'm the one who just saved the day."

"You're the one," she gritted out, "who just admitted he *watched* while Rayce got shot. What were you doing, hovering out of sight with your dragon wings, just waiting to see how all of this was going to shake down?"

"I *did* want to see what the tranq would do to the wolf." He made the confession as if it were perfectly acceptable to just hold back while someone else was hurt. But then, to him, a werewolf didn't exactly have a great deal of value.

She rose to her feet. "Screw off."

His lips parted in surprise. "That is not a thank you." He straightened his broad shoulders. "And it's not like I lingered in the air for hours or anything. I arrived just as she was pulling the gun. The bullet missed you, so I paused. Just a *pause*."

"Sometimes, a pause means death. If there had been silver in her gun and she'd hit Rayce in the heart, he would be *dead*."

His expression didn't change.

"You really are as bad as they say," she muttered, disgusted.

"I'm the *good* one."

"Keep telling yourself that." She glanced at the woman. "What did you do to her?"

"She's under my dominion. Not a bad soul, just one that was tainted by magic."

A compulsion.

"I simply put her to sleep. I figured that would be less painful than what you had planned for her."

"You know *nothing* about me."

"Sure I do…I know you hate being a vampire with every cell of your body. You think vamps are horrible monsters, just as I do. You think—"

"I think I want you out of my damn way." She glared at him. "No, scratch that...I'll *take* you out of the way." Something had just seemed to switch off inside of her at his words.

You think vamps are horrible monsters...

She ran at him, racing fast because he was standing between her and Julian. Julian was at the bottom of that snaking path, down at the dock. Julian hadn't appeared yet and he should have. That meant the human had probably tranqed him—or done something worse to him. And while Julian was suffering, Rose was wasting time with the jerk who hated her and her kind.

Before she reached him, Leo seemed to just vanish. But she felt the hot swirl of air around her and she knew he hadn't disappeared into thin air. He'd just taken flight. She didn't slow down. She raced to the dock and saw the *Devil's Prize* tied up. She jumped onto the boat.

Julian was sprawled out, his body next to Marcos. Only Julian...he seemed to have become trapped mid-shift. His bones were twisted, his limbs at odd angles. His claws were out, and faint fur lined his body.

She fell to her knees beside him.

"Julian?"

Hot air beat around her once more as her hands curled over Julian's shoulders.

ON THE PROWL

"That's…certainly interesting," Leo announced as he drew closer. "When shifters are drugged, their animals usually go out first. But with him…" He touched down onto the boat. He peered at Julian. "His panther is fighting to break free even as the man remains unconscious."

More bones popped. Snapped. The fur on Julian's body grew thicker.

"Get away from him," Leo told her, his voice sharp. "This isn't right."

"You *get* away!" She held Julian tighter. "He needs my help."

"No, that isn't what he needs." Then Leo grabbed her. She was surprised by just how strong he was—though she shouldn't have been. After all, he was just like Luke.

Or not.

He held her easily, and his wings flapped as he began to lift her into the air.

And then Julian changed completely. The panther's eyes opened and that golden gaze burned as he tilted back his head and roared. That feral stare—it locked right on her and Leo.

"*Not right,*" Leo said and he sounded worried.

The great cat leapt toward them. Leo took them higher and the panther snarled. The panther paced the boat, snarling, clawing, and roaring his displeasure.

"Let me go," Rose fought in Leo's hold. "I can help him!"

"No, you can't. His beast is in control. He's all beast, no man at all right now, and that is *not* the way this should have worked."

Leo thought he knew everything. He thought he knew Julian. He thought he knew her. Maybe it was time for him to get a wake-up call. He wasn't letting her out of his grip, just holding her with that effortless strength that was stronger than a vampire, stronger than a shifter, stronger than anything. He had one arm wrapped around her upper body, and, when she craned down her neck and chin, that arm of his was conveniently close to her mouth.

Since he wouldn't let her go...

She'd make him suffer.

Rose bit him. His blood flowed into her mouth, hot and powerful and the rush blasted through her whole body even as he bellowed in shock.

Then she was falling. He'd let her go instantly and her body hurtled through the air as she dropped fast. She wasn't like him — wings didn't magically sprout from her body. She just fell straight down and crashed into the waves. Her body sank deep as bubbles swirled around her, so thick that she couldn't see anything. Then the current was pulling at her, tossing her about, and Rose kicked up, knowing she had to get to the surface. She'd drowned before, and it was one of her least favorite ways to die.

But then there was a hand reaching out for her. Strong, hard, and it closed around her wrist, pulling her upward with an unyielding force. She kept kicking and she swam forward, following that pull. Her head broke the surface and she sucked in a deep, gasping breath.

"I've got you." Julian. Back in human form. Treading water right next to her and holding her securely in his arms. "Fucking bastard," Julian growled as he began to guide them toward the shore. "Can't believe he *dropped* you."

Julian was okay. Happiness exploded through her and she didn't even stop to think. She kissed him. Wild and frantically. She crushed her body tightly against his. She felt shock stiffen his muscles, but then he kissed her back. Julian drove his tongue past her lips, he locked his other hand around her waist, and he kissed her with the same desperation that she felt.

Some of the fear that had been inside of her lessened. That cold, clinging fear that had tightened around her heart dissipated.

The waves rocked against them.

Julian tasted like the sea.

He tasted...

His mouth pulled from hers. "Fucking scared me when I saw you fall." His words were a rumble.

"I...bit him."

His eyes widened. Then they narrowed. "What?"

There was anger in his voice. Jealousy? Too hard to say for sure. But he was holding her even tighter now and going double-time as they headed back to the shore. They didn't speak again until their feet were on the sand. He kept his hold on her wrist as they trudged up the beach.

"Where's the human?" Julian demanded. "The trigger happy one." A deep rumble vibrated his chest. His *naked* chest. Shifter side-effect. She was sure his clothes were in a ripped pile some place. "The human got aboard the *Devil's Prize*. That bitch pumped me with tranq."

Once she'd knocked Julian and Marcos out, she must have also steered the *Devil's Prize* back to shore and secured it to the dock before she'd gone hunting. But the human wasn't a threat they needed to worry about right then. "Leo put her to sleep." Rose's clothes clung to her body and water trickled over her skin. "Julian, when I first found you, it looked as if you were...caught, mid-shift. Frozen. And I was so scared..." Her words trailed away as his expression softened.

"Worried about me?" He finally freed her wrist and his hand rose so that the back of his fingers traced over her cheek. "Better tread with a fine step or you'll make me think you care."

Her chin lifted. "I don't want you dead. I've *never* wanted that."

"Then you understand, finally, how I felt the night your human life ended." His gaze glittered. "There was no fucking way I was going to let you go."

"Julian—"

"*She bit me.*" Leo's voice thundered out suddenly and she could have sworn the ground actually shook beneath her. She glanced to the left, almost expecting to see a dragon standing there, but no, Leo was still in human form. Looking incredibly pissed, but human.

"I've *never* been bitten by a vampire, not in all of my centuries on this earth." Fury twisted his face. "That's a killing offense. For someone like *her* to bite me." He waved toward Julian. "That's your job, right? *Assassin?* To take out the paranormals who cross the line. *She crossed it.* She drank from me. So take care of her."

Had he just ordered Julian to kill her?

But…

Julian didn't come at her with his claws. Instead, he moved his body, positioning himself between her and Leo. "Bugger off," he snapped at the Lord of the Light. "I don't take orders from you. You *aren't* the twin I work for, remember? And when Luke finds out that Rose took a bite out of you, he's not going to order her death.

He'll probably decide to throw her a fucking party to celebrate."

She rose onto her tip toes so that she could see over Julian's shoulders. Leo's face had mottled with fury. But she could tell...he knew Julian was right. Even she could imagine Luke's perverse joy when he found out that she'd gotten to his brother. The first vamp to get close enough to damage Mr. Holier Than Thou? Luke might even give her a medal. "It's your own fault," she told him and his eyes turned to absolute slits of fury at her words. "I wanted to get to Julian. I kept telling you to let me go."

"I was trying to help you! Ungrateful vamp!"

She shrugged. "You should have just let me go to him. He was hurting. He needed me."

But Leo shook his head. "You have *no* idea what you've done."

She'd gotten her shifter back. That was what she'd done.

"The tranqs were stronger than any I've faced before," Julian said. He didn't relax his guard for a moment, and he kept his body positioned between her and Leo. "After the last hit, I had to force my panther to the surface. I knew if there was any chance of me staying conscious, the beast had to be fully in control. But even then...it was touch and go. The panther had to claw its way out of me."

Leo was silent a moment. His face stayed tense and Rose wondered if an explosion was imminent. But then his shoulders relaxed a bit. "You are as strong as Luke always said. Now I see why he made the deal with you." His gaze slid to Rose. "Though it's not a deal I appreciate right at this moment."

"Stop being a baby," she muttered, annoyed. They had bigger problems to deal with right then.

"A what?" It sounded as if Leo were choking.

Rose barely controlled an eye roll. "It was only a few sips. Not enough to do any serious damage to you."

"It's not the damage to me I'm worried about."

What was that even supposed to mean? "Your blood wasn't that good, buddy. I get more of a rush with Julian."

His glower got worse. "I want my angel back," Leo announced. He pointed at Julian. "You were supposed to get your vamp, and stick to her like glue. Twenty-four, seven, remember? That was the deal. You were supposed to find out the identity of the Collector. You were supposed to find out where he is keeping his prisoners. You were *not* supposed to leave the vamp's side so you could get tranqed—"

"Leo, you're bossy as hell." And Julian's fingers threaded with Rose's. "Come on, love.

We're going to the house so you can get dried off and changed."

She felt a smile curve her lips. He did that a lot. Took care of her. Sure, he was primitive and scary and beast-like, but he had a different side — a protective side. One that seemed to come out with her.

They headed forward but Leo didn't get out of their path. She was pretty sure that Julian would move the guy if Leo didn't get the hint.

Leo kept glaring.

Her skin began to itch. *Weird.*

"Just so you know…" Julian drawled. "I *found* out the identity of the Collector. It's a guy named Simon Lorne. Thought he was a human at first, then I realized he's the one tossing out compulsions like candy to the mortals. That trigger happy human who pumped me full of tranqs? She was sent out here on his command. Probably because he thought we'd play nice and not hurt her."

Leo's face was a dull red. "Because you *aren't* supposed to hurt humans!"

Julian seemed to consider the situation. "Maybe she was supposed to be a distraction." He glanced out at the water, then looked back at Leo. "For all we know, Simon could be preparing to close in for the kill, and I'm not just going to stand on the beach like a welcome wagon for him. I'm getting Rose to the house and…" Now he let Rose go long enough to bound quickly over to the *Devil's Prize* and grab an unconscious Marcos from the vessel. He slung the guy over his shoulder and hurried back to Rose's side. "And I'm making sure my friends are secure. *Then* I'll hunt the bastard, just as we agreed. I'll get your angel back. I'll get all the paranormals that he's been keeping."

With Marcos still over his shoulder, Julian took Rose's hand and threaded his fingers with hers once more. "And she wasn't at my side," he rasped, "because I wanted her safe. Her safety comes first for me. *Always.* You need to remember that."

Leo took a lunging step toward him. "And *you* need to remember that if I don't get the angel back, you don't get what you wanted."

Rose rolled back her shoulders. The odd itch she felt in her skin was getting worse. And she'd started to feel...nauseous. Since when did vamps get nauseous? Well, okay, it happened...but normally only when she was hungry. When she'd gone days without blood.

They headed to the house. As they hurried up the path, they saw Rayce. A now fully awake Rayce. He had the human in his arms. She was still out cold. Good.

They'd deal with her soon enough.

Rayce whistled when he spied Leo. "This day just got even worse, didn't it?"

Leo grunted back at him.

Their little crew kept trudging to the house — a crew that now included Rayce and the human. Each step...each step became slower for Rose. Harder to take. She felt sluggish and her veins seemed heavy in her body.

Her breath came in pants. And her clothes — even though they were still wet — they felt too hot. Her skin was too hot.

She was too hot. Burning, from the inside.

"Panther." Leo's voice was flat with command. "You need to take care of the vampire."

Julian's gaze swung toward her. She tried to smile for him but...

Something is wrong with me. Something inside. She could feel it. Her heart was slowing down. Everything was slowing.

Julian put Marcos on the ground. Marcos gave a little snore. *Definitely still out.*

"Rose?" Concern flashed on Julian's face. "Rose, what's wrong?"

She tried to speak, but her throat seized up. She couldn't even gasp. Her whole body was heavy. She felt as if it were shutting down.

"I *told* you," Leo said, but his voice didn't have a know-it-all tone. Instead, he sounded worried and that scared Rose. "She drank my blood. There will be repercussions."

She was dizzy. The world spun around Rose. Julian caught her right before she fell.

"Get her inside," Leo blasted. "Give her your blood. Do whatever the hell you can for her or —"

Is my heart still beating? Rose couldn't tell.

"Or she could die…and if she does, I don't think she'll be coming back."

CHAPTER ELEVEN

"Rose? Love, love, I need you to look at me."
He tried to keep the fear out of his voice, but
Julian knew he failed. Shit, he was too terrified to
hold his control. Rose was in his arms, and she
was burning up. Literally hot to the touch—so
hot she was singing him.

She seemed to be burning up, from the inside
out, and he was so afraid that he was losing her.

*Leo should have fucking said his blood was
poison! He dicked around out there while she was
dying!*

Julian had Rose back in his room, in his
shower, and he turned on the water so that it was
ice cold. He ripped her wet clothes off her, and he
pulled her under that cold spray, desperate to do
anything to help her.

Her eyes were open, on him, but the green
was weak. Her skin was too pale, but burning
hot. She was shuddering, but not making a
sound.

She was slipping away from him.

"Drink from me," he ordered her because that had been one of Leo's orders. The guy had said she needed Julian's blood. So he'd give her every last drop if that was what it took. "Drink, love. *Drink.*"

Her little fangs were out, but she didn't move her head toward him. Instead, her head sagged forward. *No!* He drove his fingers into the thickness of her hair and tipped back her head. "You have to drink because you have to live." The water was freezing, but when it hit her body, steam rose in the air around them. He pushed her head against his neck and her teeth raked over his skin. "Bite me. Do it. *Bite.*"

Her teeth sank into him.

One of his hands slammed against the tile of the shower wall, knocking it hard enough to leave a dent. His other cradled her head, holding her so carefully. Need — dark lust — snaked through his body as it always did when she took his blood. His dick was rock hard, but he ignored the desire that came from her bite. This wasn't about sex. This was about her survival. This was about her.

She was everything to him. Had she ever realized it?

She drank. Her mouth moved on his neck, sucking him, licking, taking his blood. His muscles were rock hard. The water kept pouring onto him, but it wasn't cooling him down. When her mouth was on him, nothing cooled him down.

His fist drove into the wall again.

Stay controlled. Let her take. She needs this.

His fist hit again. He could feel the blood on his knuckles.

And his other hand tenderly cradled her.

She drank.

***

Rayce eyed the bastard who had the balls to actually saunter into the Lord of the Dark's home. "Luke is going to kick your ass."

Leo looked up — he finally stopped staring at a non-existent wound on his arm. "Only some of the stories say that is the way things end. Some of them actually say I win the battle." His lips twisted. "So maybe you need to think carefully before you go choosing sides."

"I already *have* chosen. I'm a werewolf. To you, that means I'm an animal who only knows bloodlust and death."

Leo's gaze swept over him. "How many people *have* you killed in your life?"

He wanted to kill someone right then, but he held himself back, barely. Marcos was back in his quarters, sleeping off the tranq, and the human woman — she was on the couch just a few feet away. Still lost to whatever magic Leo had used on her.

"I know what you are...rogue." Leo's eyes gleamed. "So perhaps you should have been put down long ago."

"Perhaps *you* should have been." And he'd be happy to do the job. He doubted that Leo was truly as all powerful as the guy wanted folks to think and —

"Don't you wonder why that one tranq took you out so quickly?" Leo murmured. "I mean, it took three hits for Julian to go down."

"What? Were you just fucking watching us get attacked?"

Leo pursed his lips. "I think you're actually nearly as strong as Julian — "

Nearly? That was some insulting shit. "I *am* just as strong as him."

"But there was some ingredient in the tranq that impacted you more." His head tilted to the side. "Aren't you curious about just what that ingredient is?"

Yeah, he was. Because anything that made him weak...he hated. He'd been weak before, back when he'd been a kid. Been weak and tortured and he would *never* stand for that pain again.

"Probably had silver laced in it," Rayce said, rolling back his shoulders. "Those who don't know shifters well tend to think that we all have the same weaknesses."

"Yes…they do. But, of course, silver only works on someone like you."

Wasn't he the lucky one? Rayce crossed his arms over his chest. "When the Collector found out that Rose had a shifter guarding her, he probably assumed he was facing a werewolf."

"Werewolves *are* more common."

"It was the Collector's mistake. He didn't know he was screwing with a panther." He knew Julian wouldn't give the guy a chance to make many more mistakes. And since he was thinking about Julian and just how much his buddy loved a good turn at vengeance… "Just what did you do to the vamp?"

"*I* didn't do anything. She's the one who bit me."

She bit—His eyes widened.

"She already had an…unorthodox creation. Now she has my blood in her." His gaze slid toward the door. "Maybe she'll survive."

Had he just said *maybe?* Rayce bounded across the room. His hand—with claws now at the ready—flew toward Leo's throat.

Leo didn't even flinch.

And the claws stopped less than a centimeter from Leo's jugular.

"Rose doesn't die," Rayce rasped. "Julian has already given too much to keep her in this world.

So whatever shit your blood did to her, you fix it."

"Sounds as if you care about her…"

"Only met her recently. He's my friend." Mostly. "So fix her."

"Some broken things can't be fixed. I've told that to Julian more than once."

Rayce growled. "She's not a 'broken *thing*' but you are, asshole. What is your blood doing to her?"

"It's changing her…maybe it will make her stronger. Maybe it will make her weaker. Maybe it will kill her." He shrugged and when he moved, his throat pressed to Rayce's claws. "That's why I told Julian to give her blood so that it could dilute what she'd taken from me. I am *helping*. Why is everyone so ungrateful when I do a good thing?"

He thought about cutting off Leo's head. A fast slice of his claws and —

"It wouldn't work," Leo said, as if he'd read Rayce's mind. "You'd be dead before you even tried."

Some risks were worth taking…

"I think she'll live." Leo's gaze gleamed. "This time."

The guy was such a dick.

"But if she bites me again, no one can help her."

"You *threatening* the vamp?" Julian would peel Leo's skin from his body, and Rayce would help him.

"Unfortunately, no, I'm just making a promise."

***

He should stop her. Julian's head sagged forward. The water pounded on him, and he felt himself shiver.

Rose was still drinking from him. He wasn't sure just how long they'd been in the shower. Minutes? Hours? He'd let her feed and feed, and her body wasn't blazing hot any longer.

But he...he was cold.

He should stop her. Take her out of the shower. Run a towel over her delicate skin. He should...and he would...

In a minute. He'd just give her a little more blood first.

He'd give her everything.

Only fair, wasn't it? Since he'd taken everything away from her. All in one blink. Gone, gone, gone... "S-sorry," he stuttered to her. He'd wanted to tell her before. That terrible night when the bullets had torn into her. But there had been no time for apologies. There had been no time for anything but a deal that changed both of their lives. And the damn thing was, even knowing how wrong it had been, he still thought he'd do the exact same thing.

Her tongue licked over his neck. "What for?" Her voice—it was husky and sensual. Not weak at all.

He forced his head to lift. Forced his gaze up. She wasn't pale any longer. Her eyes were bright. Her lips were red and plump and he knew she wasn't in danger. She wasn't going to die.

He pushed away from the wall. She caught his hand—the hand that he'd driven into the tile again and again, sending chunks of marble raining into the shower as he tried to hold back his dark need for her. She lifted his hand to her mouth. Licked the blood away.

His beautiful Rose. She'd chained his beast. She'd never meant to do it. She didn't even know she had.

His eyes started to close. His body slumped.

"Julian?" Alarm sharpened her voice. *"Julian!"*

He was going to pass out. Maybe he'd even die. He'd given her all that he had, given so much that his body was dangerously weak now, but Julian had no regrets. She'd survive—survive whatever hell Leo's blood had put her through. It was a fair exchange, Julian figured, considering what he'd done to her.

"No, no, no! What did I do? *What did I do?*" She held him tightly. "I took too much…you should have stopped me! Julian, why didn't you stop me?"

Didn't she know? Did she truly not understand? He tried to keep his eyes open just a moment longer.

If he was headed to hell, he wanted to take a memory of heaven with him.

"Julian?"

He tried to smile but it was too late.

CHAPTER TWELVE

"Hey, angel…"

Lila was sitting on the floor of her cell. Her wings had wrapped around her body. She was so cold. Her shivers wouldn't stop.

"What does it feel like…" The muse stood near the bars of her cell. "When he takes your feathers?"

Lila glanced at her wings. "Pain."

"Yeah, okay, I guessed that…but…*what* exactly, is the pain like?"

Lila hadn't known any pain, not until a few months ago. Now it was all she knew. The first thing she'd ever felt — pain. The thing that would forever mark her now. "For you, I imagine…it would probably be like getting chunks of your skin cut away."

"Oh, hell." The witch scrambled toward the bars of her cell. "That bad? But… you don't make a sound when he takes them."

No, she didn't. "Am I…supposed to make a sound?" She rose and moved closer to her own bars so that she could better see the other women.

The witch's voice gentled as she said, "When it hurts, it's okay to cry out."

"No!" The muse made a sharp denial. "Don't give him the satisfaction, you hear me, angel? You keep that pain inside. You don't let him hear your pain. Freaks like him get off on that. They *like* making others hurt."

She touched her wing. "Is that why he's doing all of this? Because he…likes pain?"

The muse pressed her forehead to the bars. "No. No, as crazy as this may seem, he believes what he's doing is for love."

Lila shook her head. "*This* is love?"

"It's not." The witch's voice seemed to echo around them. "I *know* love. Love is good and strong and it doesn't hurt. It makes you better. It makes everything in your whole world better."

Now the muse sighed. "Are we going to hear about your husband again?" She was mocking. She often seemed mocking. Not cruel but…not exactly kind.

The witch didn't speak.

Lila sank down onto the floor once more.

"Because I want to hear about him," the muse continued quietly. "Tell me again how your Thomas convinced you to marry him. Tell me about him again…so that before I die, I can know that at least *someone* was happy, once."

"You aren't going to die," the witch told her.

The muse laughed. "What else would he do with us? For his love to come back, you know we have to die."

They both *knew* more than she did. They'd been in their cells when she was first brought to the facility. She should question them but…she didn't want to know if death was all that waited. Not right then. "I'd like to hear more about Thomas," Lila whispered.

How long had it been since they'd had food? None of the guards ever came in to check their cells. The Collector had left strict orders that no one was to enter this domain. He'd been gone for days. If he didn't come back soon…

He will, though. He'll come back and the pain will just start again.

Her head lowered. "Tell me about love."
Because all I know is pain.

"I met Thomas when I was sixteen…" the witch began, her voice soft. "And the first thing I did was curse him."

CHAPTER THIRTEEN

Leo pressed his hand to the human's forehead. Instantly, she awoke, jerking upright and gasping.

"Nice trick," Rayce muttered, and he actually meant that.

Leo didn't look back at him. His eyes were focused on the woman — the woman who appeared increasingly terrified as her frantic stare flew around the room.

"Who are you?" she demanded. "Where am I? What's happening?"

Leo touched her forehead again. "Your name."

Rayce rocked forward on the balls of his feet. "Yeah, so, the last human that Simon got — he's still locked up in a cell, by the way — we needed vamp blood to break the compulsion that controlled him. So you might just want to hold off on the question and answer session until Rose is back in fighting form."

"I don't need Rose. Humans are under my dominion." Then Leo muttered something low —

something that sure sounded like some kind of spell. *Mind be free, respond only to me.*

Rayce's eyes narrowed.

"Tell me your name," Leo ordered.

The terror vanished from the woman's face. "Keri."

"Keri, what were you supposed to do when you reached the island?"

"Shoot anyone who wasn't Rose."

"And just who gave you that order?"

"Simon. Simon says...*find the vampire. Shoot the others...*"

Rayce was getting real sick of old Simon. "How'd she know what Rose even looked like?"

Keri blinked. "I saw her picture. He showed me, on his phone."

Rayce's hand raked over his face. "Right. Of course. His freaking phone."

"I was supposed to call him if she's here." Her words tumbled out quickly, easily, as if she *had* to speak them. "Simon says he'll fly in. Simon says they won't hurt me. I'm human... They won't hurt me."

"See?" Leo glanced back at Rayce, smirking. "I told you, she's under my dominion. I can control—"

"*Simon says death.*" And the little human had just yanked a knife from her boot. "*Simon says kill if anyone gets in my way.*" She drove the knife straight at Leo. Blood flew from his neck, but when she came at him again, he knocked the knife from her hand.

It clattered across the floor.

"*Sonofabitch.*" Leo glared at the woman.

Her face was slack once more. "*Simon says kill.*"

Rayce wouldn't let himself smile. Oh, hell, why not? It was his turn to smirk as he said, "You should really consider waiting on Rose. That vamp blood might come in handy after all."

Leo grabbed the woman's arms and pulled her up. "*Mind be free, respond only to me.*"

"Yeah, that didn't work so well the first time…"

But Leo ignored him. "Tell me the plan. When you find Rose, what are you supposed to do?"

She blinked her wide, blue eyes. "Don't have to do anything. He's already coming…I already told him she was here. Saw her from my boat." And then Keri smiled. "*Simons says…we will all die.*"

***

"Julian?" She had him on the bed. He'd stumbled out of the shower with her then collapsed on the mattress. His eyes were closed and he barely seemed to be breathing…and he was *terrifying* her. "Julian, wake up."

Her shaking fingers pressed to his throat. The wounds she'd made with her bite were still there. They usually faded—he usually healed so quickly.

But he'd been tranqed today. And I…I took too much.

Guilt ate at her soul. She knew she'd taken too much. But she'd been caught in some kind of firestorm. She'd seen herself from a distance, and she hadn't been able to stop. She'd fed and fed and the fire inside of her had demanded more. It had demanded that she keep taking. *Taking.* Until nothing was left.

A tear slid down her cheek. She brushed her mouth against his. "I'm sorry." She'd hurt him. But she could make this right. He was still breathing. His heart beat…it was just slow. *I have to make this right.* She bit her wrist and then forced it to his mouth. He'd take her blood and he *would* get stronger. It had worked before for them. It would work again.

"Julian, drink."

She kept her hand shoved against his mouth. Her blood trickled inside his mouth, but he wasn't swallowing. She was straddling his body, and while she kept one wrist at his mouth, her other massaged his throat, forcing him to swallow. She *made* him take her blood. She wasn't just going to watch him die on her. That wasn't ever going to happen—

Oh, my God.

As she just realized what she'd thought, her heart stopped.

I can't watch him die...just like he couldn't watch me die.

Then his eyes flew open. Julian's stare burned with power — with the force of his beast. His golden eyes were glowing and she felt his canines lengthening. Then *he* was biting her. His hand flew up and held tightly to her wrist, forcing her even closer to him. He bit, he drank, and he...

"More." His hands curled around her and he brought her down closer to him, putting her neck right in front of his mouth. "I want to taste more." And he bit her again, this time, right on the curve of her neck and the pleasure/pain of that bite had her hips rocking against him.

She was naked and so was he. She rocked against him, pushing her neck closer to him, pushing her sex against him, and the friction just made her desire mount.

For vamps, bloodlust and physical lust always went hand in hand. The more blood you took, the harder your lust burned. The hotter. The darker.

Her hand pushed between them. His cock sprang toward her, fully erect and ready. Thick. Hard. She wanted him *in* her. She wanted his teeth in her neck and his cock in her body. She lifted up her hips, positioning him even as he continued to drink, and then she came down on him, taking him all the way inside and gasping because he felt so good.

So right.

Her desires were darker now. She never would have thought drinking and fucking were a combination she wanted. She never would have thought her dream lover was a man with a savage side.

She'd been thinking all wrong for far too long.

His hand slid down her body, his claws were out and he raked her skin — didn't hurt her, but he had her gasping and arching toward him. She was so sensitive and he touched her — he touched her *everywhere*.

His mouth slid from her neck. He nuzzled her again. "Never letting go…" His gaze glowed at her. "Remember that." A warning.

Then…

Then she felt his control shatter. His hips withdrew, then slammed hard against her. The bed jerked beneath them. A feral growl came from him and he rolled her on the bed. He trapped her beneath him, yanked her legs up high so they were over his shoulders…

And he took.

And she took.

And they both moaned at the raw pleasure. His thrusts sent his cock over her clit, every fierce drive heightening her need. Her nails raked down his back and she didn't use the care he had. She *wanted* to mark him. He was hers, and she wasn't letting go. Her nails sank into his skin. He laughed and thrust even harder.

"Mine." His word, but it could have been hers. That moment was so primitive, so basic. It was a claiming. An owning, and there was no going back.

He'd given her his blood.

She'd given him hers.

He'd taken her body.

And she wanted his heart.

The release hit her first, blasting through her and sending pleasure bursting inside of her. Her sex spasmed around him, contracting against his cock, and she felt his release as he surged hotly inside of her. When he came, he kissed her, thrusting his tongue past her lips, and she swore she could taste his pleasure. Her heart thundered in her chest, her body quaked, and Julian was all she could feel and see. Julian with his bright eyes, his feral smile. Julian, with his beast inside.

Her beast.

Her Julian.

Hers.

And that thought was utterly terrifying. She'd spent so much time running from the one man that she wanted most…because he was the one man who held the power to destroy her completely. He'd done it before. Could she trust him never to do it again?

CHAPTER FOURTEEN

A sharp knock sounded at Julian's door. "If you two are done in there..." Rayce's voice bellowed. "I need your asses out, ASAP. I've got a pissed off Lord of the Light down here...and a human who could seriously use some vamp blood."

"I'm going to kill him," Julian muttered as he raised up onto his forearms.

But Rose smiled. "No, you're not. You care about him. You don't kill those you care about."

If only that were true. "You don't know panthers." He pulled from her body, hating to let her go, but knowing there wasn't a choice. Rayce's footsteps had retreated, but he couldn't ignore reality — and his reality was currently one big nightmare.

A faint furrow appeared between Rose's brows. "You're right. I don't know panther shifters. You're the only one I've ever met. So maybe you should tell me...what am I missing?"

He stalked to his closet and yanked out a pair of jeans. A t-shirt. He dressed quickly, his movements tight and jerky. He grabbed a pair of shoes—

"Julian?"

He looked back. She was standing by the bed, naked, her body a perfect temptation. He would have loved to get her back in that bed. To get her under him. Over him. To spend hours tasting every single inch of her.

But the danger wasn't going to wait.

"You want to know about us? We're brutal. Savage. When we attack, there is no other beast that can match us. Our favorite way to kill?" His voice sounded cold. He felt cold. "We stalk our prey, never making a sound. We kill large prey — prey like other paranormals or…humans—with a bite to the back of the neck. That bite severs the spinal cord, so there is no chance for the prey to fight back."

She didn't make a sound. He raked a hand over his face. Enough fucking sharing. "Panthers are brutal. We're beasts to our core. And *that's* what you really need to understand."

"I think…I think there is more to you than that."

Then you're wrong. He dropped his hand. "How are you feeling?" he asked, and his voice was still cold. Cold and curt, but that was just how he sounded, not how he really felt. Looking at her…he felt good right then because Rose *appeared* okay. No, she looked way better than okay.

"I don't feel like I'm burning up from the inside, so I figure that's a good sign." She made no move to cover her body because, obviously, she liked causing him pain. "What about you?" And the furrow between her brows deepened. "You're the one who got drained dry." She stepped toward him. "Why? You should have stopped me. You had to know I was taking too much. You got so weak—"

"For all I knew, Leo's blood was poisoning you." *Killing you.* "I had to make sure you survived, and the more of my blood I gave you...hell, I thought it might dilute whatever was in his. I just wanted..." He heaved out a breath. "I had to make sure you were all right."

Her hands lifted and pressed to his chest. "I was out of control. I could have *killed* you."

"It wasn't that close."

Her gaze searched his. "You're a liar."

"Only every day..." He turned from her, went into his closet, and pulled out clothes that he knew would fit her. He handed them to her. "Don't want you walking into the room nude when we see Leo and Rayce again."

She looked down at the clothes, then up at him. "Okay, this is the second time you've pulled out clothes for me." Her head cocked. "Which means…you keep women's clothes in your closet?"

"Cute. I keep clothes for you in there, okay? Don't make a big deal out of it."

But Rose shook her head. "For me?"

"Yeah, shit, I had some stuff on hand, okay? Just in case…"

"Just in case — what?" Rose prompted. "I wound up naked on the island?"

"Just in case I was ever lucky enough to have you back," the words exploded and he could feel his cheeks heating. He cleared his throat and tried to sound a bit calmer as he said, "I wanted to make sure you had what you needed. It's not a big deal."

"You're lying again. I think I can tell now when you do…"

"Because my mouth is moving?" He needed to get away from her. The blood exchange — the sex — *the mating*. It had all been too intense, and she didn't even realize the ramifications of what had just gone down. Mostly because he hadn't told her.

More lies. Shit. He should have told her what it meant for him to take her blood — for him to bite her neck and her shoulder. And he hadn't just done that mating bite once — oh, no, this was the *second time* he'd marked her that way.

She had no clue what he'd done. He should tell her. Right then. But he…he didn't want to change the way she was looking at him. Some of the tension was gone from her gaze. Her expression seemed softer. As if she might be…hell, maybe thinking about giving him another chance.

Too bad he'd already screwed that chance up for them.

Julian marched for the door. "When you're dressed, join us." He stopped and glared back at her. "Seriously, when you are *dressed*. If you walk out naked, I'll have to knock Rayce unconscious."

"I don't…understand you."

What wasn't to understand? "When it comes to you, I'm a jealous bastard. Always have been. I…consider you mine." That was as close to an admission about the marking and mating as he could get right then.

Her lips parted.

"Because you are." Truth. The biggest truth he'd ever given her.

"Julian—"

"Get dressed." He yanked open the door and hurried into the hallway. Julian tried to breathe without tasting her, but she was in his blood — literally. Under his skin. Branded on his soul. He stomped his way down the hallway and joined the others and when Rayce took a look at his face, he winced.

"Tell me it's not that bad," Rayce ordered.

"It's worse." Because he'd mated with her — mated *for life* – and she had no clue. He'd let his beast go, their blood had melded, and there was no going back. At least, there was no going back for him. But a mating only worked for a shifter. He would be tied to her forever, but Rose didn't *have* to know. She wouldn't be forced to feel the same connection that he did. She could be free.

While he was trapped in hell without her.

"How could it be worse?"

His gaze cut to Leo and he gave a little growl. This wasn't sharing time, especially not with Leo and the wide-eyed human watching them. Rayce got the message and gave a little nod. Finally. Exhaling, Julian glanced over at the woman who sat on the couch. The trigger-happy one. He rubbed his chin and she paled. Julian frowned. "Is that blood on her shirt?"

Coughing a bit, Rayce said. "Yes, there was an...altercation."

Leo's face hardened. "I don't have time for this crap. Get the vamp in here, let's break the compulsion, then we are going after the angel."

"Jeez, man, I get that you want your girlfriend back, but chill out." Rayce shook his head. "Despite what Julian here may have led you to believe, you can't go around thinking with your dick."

"She *isn't* my girlfriend," Leo snapped. "Lila is an angel. Don't you get what that even means?

She's never known pain. Never known hate. Never known rage."

Rayce's face went dark. "Good fucking deal for her. Maybe she's long *overdue* then—"

"No!" Leo roared. "She's never known them because she'd feel them too intensely. A thousand times worse than what it would be like for a human—a hundred times worse than what it would be like for someone like you." His shoulders sagged. "It will break her. Splinter her mind. Drain who she is until *all* that she has is the darkness of that pain. She will be lost, and when an angel is lost..." He licked his lips. "The whole world suffers for it."

Silence.

Julian's gaze slid to the doorway. He'd heard Rose coming down the hallway. He'd been tuned to her even as Leo spoke.

"Well...from the sound of things..." Rose squared her shoulders. "It seems we have an angel to save."

"An angel, a muse, and who the hell knows what else." Julian didn't move toward Rose.

"Sounds like the start of a really bad joke," Rayce cut in. "An angel, a muse, and a werewolf walk into a bar—"

"*This isn't a joke!*" Leo bellowed. "She's *dying*. Lila will lose her wings and then there will be no going back. I get that you two don't care about her pain." He cast a dismissive glance toward

Julian and Rayce. "But what about you?" Leo
stared at Rose. "Don't you care that an innocent is
suffering? You've been imprisoned before.
You've been tortured. How can you just let
another woman suffer that way?"

Julian saw the sympathy fill Rose's eyes. "I
can't," she said. "I will help them. I swear —"

"Rose —" Julian thundered.

Too late.

Leo grabbed her hand. "Deal. A promise is a
promise." A faint light appeared above their
joined hands. Julian knew exactly what that light
meant. *A sealed deal.*

Rose pulled back her hand and stared down
at her palm. "What just happened?"

"You made a deal," Leo told her. "You
promised to help."

Rayce surged to her side. "And you promised
nothing to her! What in the hell kind of deal is
that supposed to be?"

But Leo's gaze cut to Julian. "Not true. I've
already promised plenty." He nodded, once,
hard, as if satisfied, then he turned his stare back
to Rose. "Now, go give the human your blood.
Break her compulsion tie and get her to tell us
what's happening next."

"Please," Rose muttered.

Leo frowned at her.

"You can at least say *please* instead of bossing
everyone around. It makes you look a lot less like

an asshole." She headed toward the woman on the couch. Rose brought her hand to her mouth and bit into her wrist. For a moment, her gaze darted toward Julian, and he knew she was remembering all that they'd just done.

He clenched his jaw when her gaze darted away. She put her hand to the lady's mouth, forcing her to drink.

"So how long will this take?" Leo demanded, impatience written on his face. "Because we need to know—"

"What does Simon have planned?" Rose asked as she stared into the other woman's eyes. "Tell me."

"Uh, her name is Keri," Rayce offered helpfully. "We learned that already. You know, before that deep compulsion reared its ugly head and she tried to slice open Leo. Not that I blame her, not even a little bit."

Leo glared at him. "We are going to have issues."

"We already do."

Rose seemed to ignore them as she focused on the woman before her. "Tell me, Keri," she encouraged. "Tell me what Simon Lorne is going to do."

Keri's expression had gone slack. "Your guards will be unconscious." Her voice was slow, husky. "Either they killed me when they saw me…or they let me pass, thinking I was just a lost human."

Rayce started pacing. "*This* is why humans can't be trusted." He pointed to Leo. "You think they're these innocent lambs. They aren't."

"I was to shoot them," Keri continued quietly. "Give them the tranq. Then shoot you. When you were all out, I was going to wait for Simon to come for us."

Julian saw a trickle of blood slide down from Rose's wrist.

Rose lifted a brow. "Can't help but note…Simon *isn't here.* Were you supposed to call him?"

Keri nodded. "I called him from the boat. Radioed him when I saw you on the beach."

"Then why isn't he already storming the island?" Rose shook her head. Her brow crinkled. "He must have seen something…something that made him hesitate. He had to rethink his little master plan and —" She whirled and pointed her index finger at Leo. "He saw you."

Leo's eyes widened. He looked offended. He looked…guilty.

"Hard to miss a guy with giant wings flying through the air," she snapped. "When you grabbed me and flew up into the air, he must have been watching. It fits the timeline Keri just gave us. She tipped him off, he would have started closing in — since he'd gotten confirmation of my location—but then you pull your dragon routine and he backed off. The guy could be running right now, going away far and fast *because of you!*"

Keri shuddered. "Did you say...d-dragon?"

Rose didn't glance back at her. "We can't just stand here and keep waiting. Keep hiding. If you want to rescue the others, then we're doing it." She nodded decisively. "But on *my* terms. Got it? Because it's my deal now."

The guilt was gone from Leo's face. "I don't think you understand who it is that you're talking to."

"I don't really give a shit who you think you are. All I care about...well, it's that we work together on this. I said I'd help find those other paranormals, and that's what I'm going to do." She cast a quick glance over her shoulder, peering back at Julian. "Though you might not like all my methods..."

"Rose..." Julian began, voice grim.

"We're going to take the *Devil's Prize*, and we're going back to Key West." Her shoulders were squared, her spine straight, her chin up. "We think Simon has a base somewhere in the Everglades, right? So we need to get him to show us his hiding spot."

"What do you think I've been *trying* to do?" Leo snarled as he threw his hands into the air.

"You haven't been trying with the right bait."

Julian bounded toward Rose. He caught her shoulder and spun her around to face him. "No. *No.*"

She smiled. "Yes. *Yes.*"

A growl broke from him.

"I'm not the damsel in distress, Julian."

What the fuck? Who'd ever said she was?

"I'm not the woman who gets to hide from the dark. I see all of that now. I *am* the dark. I'm the vampire. I'm the bad thing that others should fear."

She wasn't bad. That was the problem. She'd always been good, straight to her soul. Far too good for someone like him. He'd known that truth the instant he met her, but he hadn't been able to stay away.

"I'm the thing *he* should fear. Simon thinks he's going to *collect* me? Terrorize me? Hurt my friends? No, this is ending. He wants me…" Her smile flashed, showing her white, sharp fangs. "Then he's going to get me."

He *hated* this plan. His hands fell away from her.

"He's going to get us all," she added.

His eyes narrowed. "I'm listening." And maybe he was liking the plan a bit more. If they were *all* attacking.

She inclined her head toward Keri—a Keri who'd gone white and appeared to be suffering from shock. Learning about dragons probably did that to a human. "She and I will go out on the *Devil's Prize*. You and Rayce will be below deck. You two will stay out of sight...I figure that's something you guys excel at, right? Shifters are good at sneaking around."

Of course. They knew how to hunt without making a sound.

"And Leo...he can cover us from above. Provided, of course, that he can go up *high* enough that his ass won't be spotted again by Simon."

Leo sniffed. "We don't *know* he spotted me before. Maybe he just decided to back off when he saw your panther lover dive into the water after you. Not every day that a full-sized black panther decides to take a swim in the ocean."

Only he hadn't been a panther when he'd found her. He'd shifted beneath the water and saved her as a man.

"We get on the boat," she continued doggedly, "and Keri contacts him again on the radio. She tells him that she's bringing me in...she gets a meet site set up."

Leo smiled. "And then we show up and grab the bastard."

"Give me patience," she muttered. Rose squeezed her eyes shut. "I get that you *think* you can make the guy talk, but what if you can't?" Her eyes opened. "What if Simon won't reveal the location of the others? What if he keeps them there, locked away, no matter *what* you do to him?"

"I have dominion over all humans—"

"We don't know he *is* human," she said, her voice rising. "And since we don't know *what* he is, then we don't even know if I can put him under a compulsion or if you can control him. So we can't just grab the guy and force the location out of him."

Julian knew where she was going with this plan, and he was back to hating it. "You want to offer yourself up—get him to take you and lock you up with the others."

Her smile hurt his heart. "When he takes me with him, you all follow. Easy enough, right? I mean..." Now her hand lifted to press against his chest, right over his heart. "You're a shifter. Doesn't that mean you can follow my scent anywhere?"

He'd mated them. He could follow her *anywhere*, could locate her no matter where she went on this Earth. Julian gave a curt nod.

"Then you follow. We find the hole Simon has been hiding inside, and you guys storm the place." Her voice had hardened with determination. "We take out Simon. We free the others, and then all of the deals are done."

"What happens to me?" Keri whispered. "Can I please go home?"

Rose swallowed. "Yes. You'll go home. You'll go home and so will Francis. Neither one of you will even remember what happened. You can go right back to your lives and forget Simon."

"I'd like to forget." A tear slid down Keri's cheek. "I'd like that very much."

Because she didn't want to know about the monsters in the world. Rose had been that way, once.

But her blinders were long gone.

"Gentleman." Rose clapped her hands together. "Do we have a plan?" Her gaze swept them all. "Or are we just going to keep hiding out on this island while Simon decides that he wants to collect other paranormals? While he imprisons more beings?"

Leo nodded, grudgingly. "We have a plan."

"I'm in," Rayce said at once. "Not like I have anything else better to do. And I sure as hell want to pay the guy back for that tranq." He fired a smile Leo's way. "Besides, I've never seen an angel before. Hoping she lives up to my expectations."

Leo raked him with a stare. "Don't even think it. She plays in a league you'll never be able to touch."

Rayce just laughed.

Rose's stare slid back to Julian. "What about you? Are you in?"

In on a plan that risked her life? That let a sadistic sonofabitch get his hands on her?

"I need to know I can count on you." Her gaze searched his. "Because I *am* doing this. I've been captive before. I've been locked away. Someone has to get the others out. And this time, I'm that someone. I'm the one who rides to the rescue and I want you riding with me."

"When you want me there, I will always be at your side." There was no other place he'd rather be. Didn't she get that?

Her breath sighed out. "Thank you."

She didn't need to thank him. Not for a damn thing. Rose started to turn away, but he caught her arm and pulled her close. His head leaned toward hers. "If you get hurt...if you get so much as a scratch, I'm ripping Simon apart."

Her gaze held his. "If you get hurt...if you get so much as a scratch, *I'm* ripping Simon apart."

He smiled. Fuck, but she made him feel good.

"Blood-thirsty, isn't she?" Leo muttered.

"*She's* a vamp," Rose called out. "What the hell else did you expect me to be?" Then she leaned up and pressed a kiss to Julian's lips. "Thanks for having my back."

Always.

She slipped from his arms and headed for the door. "Let's do this."

Rayce saluted and followed her out—after he stopped to toss the human female over his shoulder. Julian stalked after them, but Leo stepped into his path. "The angel is my priority."

The guy was such a dick. "And the others what—they don't matter at all?"

"Lila is one of mine. If she isn't off this plane soon, there *will* be no going back for her. She wasn't meant to live with humans…or with beasts."

"Now you're just being insulting." Julian gave him a hard grin. "Want to know *my* priority?"

"I already do. It's the vamp who just walked out. Only she's seeming a whole lot less and less like the innocent girl you fell for, isn't she? Turning into a real vamp right before our eyes." Leo's face was hard. "Time's running out for her, too. You keep up your end of the deal, and I'll still keep up mine. I can change her. I can give her back everything that you took away."

Because that had been the original deal he'd made with Leo. He'd known that Rose hated what she was, and he'd wanted to give her a choice.

When he hadn't before.

"If this goes to hell, get the angel out first," Leo ordered.

Screw that. If this went to hell, he'd be grabbing Rose first. She was *his* priority.

"Do it, and I'll owe you," Leo added.

"Buddy, you better just get the fuck out of this house. When Luke comes back and he finds your stench all over the place, he's gonna be pissed."

Leo didn't appear concerned. "Do we have a deal?" He offered his hand.

Julian didn't take it. "I'll do my part when the time comes." That was all he'd say. Rose—she was his part. She was his everything. "But I do have one question…" Something that was nagging at him.

Leo lifted a brow.

"You told me that one of the Collector's guards had managed to escape…that *he'd* been the one to warn you that Rose was next on the target list."

"Yes, yes that's what happened."

"But then you said he died before he could reveal Lila's location to you."

Leo's lips thinned.

"I think you told me that he burned, from the inside out." He raised one brow. "Never heard of that happening before but then…when Rose bit you, when she had *your* blood inside of her, she seemed to be burning from the inside out, too."

A muscle flexed in Leo's jaw. "I don't hear a question. Just a panther rambling."

He grabbed the guy's shoulders and let his claws cut into the skin. "*You* killed the guard, didn't you?"

Leo glanced down at Julian's claws, then back up at his face.

"The guy didn't turn because of the angel. She didn't work her magic on him. You found the guy, you knew he was tied to the Collector, and you tried to make him tell you where the angel was."

"You should move those claws."

"And you should stop dicking around!" He let the claws sink deeper. "What went wrong? Was it another one of those deeply buried compulsions? Did your power not work on the human because of it? He could hold out against your power so you killed him?"

"He tried to kill me. I had no choice."

But Julian had to laugh at that. "There's always a choice, mate. We just don't make the right ones." He knew that from bitter experience. "Don't lie to me again, got it? Not when Rose's life is on the line. I don't care about your angel. I only care about her."

"Obviously," Leo drawled. "But it's not my fault your vamp was just at death's door. I never told her to drink my blood." His eyes gleamed. "And if you want to keep her with you, then I'd suggest you make sure she never gets the urge to bite around me again."

Maybe he should just take the guy's head right then and there —

"I say that as a warning. Sometimes what doesn't kill us the first time...it takes us out even faster the second." Leo inclined his head to Julian. "Remember that."

"Hey!" Rayce called out. "You assholes coming or what?"

Julian retracted his claws.

Leo spun away and marched into the hallway. Julian followed but stopped short when he saw Rayce — still holding the human. He knew Rayce had overheard his little chat with Leo. Rayce shook his head. "You are playing a dangerous game."

"Those are the only games I like."

And they were the games that he *had* to win.

***

"Sir? You're being hailed on the radio."

The helicopter flew over the water, heading back for the landing pad. Simon needed to fucking regroup after the shit he'd seen.

*The vamp isn't getting away. I just have to get rid of her protectors...*some very unusual protectors.

"It's the woman you sent. Keri."

He blinked. She was still alive? "Patch her through to my headset."

And a moment later...

"*S-Simon?*" He instantly recognized her shaking voice. "You said...said you would come."

"Change of plans." *Why* was she still alive?

"I...have the vampire."

He stared down at the water below him. Then he picked up his binoculars and gazed into the distance. He saw a boat zipping across the waves.

"I drugged them all...and she's on the boat with me. I'm-I'm coming back to you."

Wasn't that interesting? "And the others are all on the island? *Tell me, Keri. Tell me where they are.*"

Silence. Then... "Wh-where are you?"

She can't tell me a lie. That was part of the compulsion he'd planted deep within her mind.

So he thought over the words she'd said to him. *I drugged them all.* Truth. She had. But...

Were they still unconscious someplace? Or were they out, hunting?

And...as for the vampire...*she's on the boat with me.* Another truth. Only Keri hadn't said that Rose was unconscious, just that she was on the boat.

He smiled. *I smell a trap.* How very creative. Did they think he'd just waltz right up to them like a lamb to the slaughter? "I'll meet you on Key West. Head for the south end dock. I'll be there." Then he motioned to end the connection. The helicopter buzzed through the air.

He had come prepared this time. Humans weren't the only ones that he knew how to use. He took off his headphones and glanced back at the man behind him. "Retrieve the vampire. I'll meet you back at base."

The man nodded. Then he moved toward the helicopter's door. He yanked it open and air whooshed into the chopper. The wind beat against the suit that the fellow wore. He stared down below for a moment, looking at the waves.

And then he jumped.

Simon smiled. The guy had been his first experiment — and he was still one of Simon's favorites.

CHAPTER FIFTEEN

Leo made sure that he stayed out of sight.
His wings flapped in the air, carrying him easily.
Not that he believed he'd been spotted by Simon
Lorne before...but...okay, perhaps he had.

But he'd been trying to help. Not that the
dark paranormals had appreciated his efforts.
They never did.

Just like his brother Luke never appreciated
anything he did. Luke lived by his own rules,
tending to just feel as if the rest of the world
could go fuck off.

It couldn't. That wasn't the way things
worked.

His eyes swept the water below him. The
Devil's Prize was making its way to the Key West
dock, moving at a fast clip. Rose was hauling ass.
He almost smiled, but then he remembered he
wasn't supposed to like vampires.

Only she wasn't ever meant to be a vampire.
Such a sad situation—

Something hit him. Something that felt like a
giant, freaking stone. It slammed into him and he

felt his right wing tear as he plummeted downward. Leo tried to fight, but he was held in an unbreakable grip. Stronger than anything he'd ever faced before.

He roared his fury and let the change sweep through him, a full-on transformation that he rarely allowed because he knew it was too dangerous. Thick, sharp scales broke through his skin, a long, winding tail snapped out from his body and —

"Can't have that." A voice that was a thick rumble. "You're done."

His gaze craned toward the man who'd attacked him. Only it wasn't a man. It was a monster — half stone, half winged devil. All nightmare. And it was *so strong*.

"Done," his attacker said again as he drove Leo straight down, sending the Lord of the Light crashing beneath the waves of the ocean.

***

"This is the end for you, Keri." Rose put her hand on the other woman's shoulder. They'd just docked and she knew that Simon would be showing soon. *That means it is time for the human to get away.* Keri blinked and stared up at her. "I want you to walk away from the dock. I want you to go back to your home and I want you to *forget* everything you learned about Simon and paranormal creatures."

Keri stared up at her.

"Monsters aren't real." Rose forced a smile. "Tell me that."

"Monsters aren't real," Keri repeated.

"Remember that. And go have a great, *normal* life, okay?"

Keri nodded, and then, without another word, she headed off the boat. She jumped onto the dock and landed easily. She didn't look back as she left.

Rose's shoulders sagged. One problem down. Hopefully. She bit her lower lip as she glanced around nervously. When would Simon be showing? Julian and Rayce were below deck, probably prowling like caged tigers, but they knew the drill.

Do not show yourselves. Not yet.

She heard the whoosh of wind picking up and her gaze shot upward. Hell. What part of *low profile* had Leo not understood? Seriously, if he messed this up for them again…

That's not Leo.

A giant beast slammed into the boat—a beast that was a terrible combination of man and stone. Huge wings spread from his back. His face was distorted, his teeth enormous, and his blue eyes…

They blazed.

"Collecting you," he rasped.

The boat shuddered beneath his weight.

She didn't know who that guy was but…he was obviously Simon's errand boy. She just hadn't expected such a *large* errand boy. Or one with such big claws. And teeth. And massive wings.

And one made of *stone*. "What are you?" Rose whispered as she backed up.

He took a sliding step toward her.

Fear stole her breath.

***

"Something is wrong," Julian said as his gaze shot upward. Someone—something—had just landed on the boat with a thud—and with enough force to send the whole boat rocking. He inhaled and his body tensed as he caught the new scents in the air. *Brimstone. Magic. Fear.* "Rose is afraid." He lunged for the stairs that would take him above deck.

Rayce grabbed his shirt. The material tore. "Shit, man, wait! You know the plan! She's *supposed* to get taken."

He snarled at his friend. "*She's afraid.*"

"That kind of goes along with the whole *getting* taken part. We knew this was going to happen. Now man up and do your job. We'll track her. We'll find the others. We'll kill the freaking *Collector* — "

But a scream had just cut through Rayce's words. Rose's scream. And the boat rolled hard again. It shuddered — and the thing begin to sink.

He and Rayce both ran up the stairs. They exploded onto the deck to see that the place was being wrecked. Destroyed by a big, stone beast.

"Oh, fuck no," Rayce said. "Tell me I'm not staring at —"

A gargoyle. He was — they were both staring at the massive figure of a stone gargoyle. One of the worst shifters out there.

And the bastard launched into the air, holding Rose tightly in his arms.

"No!" Julian bellowed.

"Relax." Rayce slapped a hand against him. "You've seriously got to chill out. We knew someone would come for her. Granted, I don't think we expected *that* guy…"

Gargoyles were supposed to be extinct. *Fucking hell.*

"It's all right. We've got this." Rayce sounded far too confident. "The plan is working just as she said. They took the bait."

The gargoyle had taken *her.*

"Now we hunt…" Rayce glanced around the rapidly filling boat. "And we get out of here before we have to take a swim."

Julian bounded off the boat. No humans were around, so they'd missed the whole freaking *gargoyle* show. And that gargoyle, it was moving helluva fast. Already the thing was a mere speck in the sky.

"Leo is up there," Rayce said, still sounding too confident. "He'll have the guy in his sights." But then he shook his head. "*Gargoyle.* How the hell did that guy get involved in this mess? And how is he even alive? I thought the witches took out the last of them centuries ago. I mean, shit, I remember the old wars...the witches cursed the knights to change. They were shifters not born but made and..." His words stumbled to a stop. "Oh, damn."

Not born but made. Just as Rose was a vampire who hadn't been born but made. She hadn't been created through a bite—but by magic. *Just like a gargoyle.*

"I think we might have been missing a few things with the Collector." Rayce wasn't sounding so confident any longer. "A few other things that good old Leo neglected to mention to us. Like, you know, the fact that the Collector had a gargoyle at his beck and call."

Julian's nostrils flared. "We need to track, *now.*"

"I told you, Leo has sights on them, he has—"

The water erupted to their right as Leo shot up from the waves. A drenched, bleeding Leo. "Freaking gargoyle," he muttered as he slammed onto the dock.

Rayce closed his eyes and squeezed the bridge of his nose. *"Shit."*

"It's okay." Julian rolled back his shoulders and let his claws slide out. "I can track Rose. I can *always* track her now."

Shock flashed on Rayce's face. "Oh, no, man, tell me you didn't. Tell me you —"

"I can always find what's mine." He marched toward the small building that waited to the right — Luke's building, the one the guy used to store their vehicles for use on Key West. Julian unlocked the door with a quick twist of his hand. His motorcycle was waiting inside, exactly where he'd left it when he and Rose had first gone sneaking toward the *Pandora*. Two other top-of-the-line motorcycles were nearby. And a dozen other high-end cars. "Pick your poison," Julian said. Then he jumped on his motorcycle. Moments later, he was revving the engine. "And try to keep up."

***

The stone beast flew to the ground, and his grip never eased on Rose. When he hit the earth, she heard the heavy thud of impact, and she was pretty sure the ground sank a few inches beneath his weight.

Her breath heaved out of her lungs and her heart raced in her chest. She looked up at him, wondering what would happen next. There was only one word for that guy...scary. He was so beyond anything she'd seen before.

He put Rose on her feet. "Don't...run." When he spoke, his voice was deep and echoing.

Run? Where was she supposed to run to, exactly? Rose risked a look around — she was in the swamp. No, the Everglades. When they'd flown, she'd looked down and noted the saw grass marshes and mangrove forests — stretching for miles. She'd seen the snaking wetlands. She'd seen the gators. She'd heard the cry of a million insects.

Her captor roared and her gaze shot back to him — only to realize that he'd completely turned to stone. No more weird half-man, half-stone combination. He was pure stone. She inched forward, lifting her hand to touch him because he appeared to be a giant, snarling statue.

Just when her fingers were about to tap against the stone, a man's hand broke through the statue.

She jerked her own hand back, jumping a bit.

Then his second hand broke free. As she watched, he smashed his way free of the stone. Soon the beast was gone, and a man stood in his place. Tall, muscled, with dark brown hair and blue eyes. And naked. Because, of course, wasn't that the way with shifters? And this fellow...he was definitely *some* kind of shifter, just a kind she hadn't seen before.

"You...didn't run." His voice wasn't quite so thundering now. Still deep but, not *beast-mode* deep.

"Why would I run?"

He raised one brow. "Because you were just kidnapped by a gargoyle?"

"Is that what you are?" She studied him again. Yes, it fit. "Interesting."

He grunted. Then he caught her wrist in his hand. "You should have run."

"But I'm in the middle of nowhere. And I haven't gotten what I came for."

The guy slanted a wary glance her way. "What's that?"

"The others. I'm ending his collection."

His gaze hardened. "He's going to end you."

The words didn't really sound like a threat. More like a sad fact. The guy even looked sad in that moment. But he was still dragging her through the Everglades. They cleared a particularly vicious twisting path and then...

She saw it. The hidden base. No, not a base, a prison.

"It used to be a government research facility," he said, his grip hard on her. "Guess it still is...only the research isn't quite so scientific any longer."

She counted two armed guards at the entrance to the facility. It was a long and squat building, snaking back toward the tall grass. There was a helipad to the right, and a chopper sat there, its blades still moved gently, as if it had only recently landed.

"I'm sorry," he said.

Rose blinked, certain she'd misheard. "Why?"

His smile was cold. "Because it's going to hurt...and you're going to die."

No, I'm not. Julian is coming. Everyone is getting out of here. "I think you chose the wrong team."

"I never chose anything."

"Trust me, buddy, I know the feeling."

He frowned.

Before he could speak again, the doors to the building opened. A blond man strode out, a grin stretching from ear to ear.

"My last piece!" Simon cried out. "How absolutely wonderful!" He rushed toward her, and she almost expected him to rub his hands in glee. "And you just offered yourself up to me. I mean, does my luck get any better?"

No, it only gets worse.

A whole lot worse.

"Take her inside," he barked to the men with guns. "And you..." He pointed to the gargoyle. "Kill anyone who comes after her."

A gargoyle against a panther…stone against claws and teeth…. "Wait," Rose began. "Don't—"

The guard on the right lifted his gun. The bastard *fired* it at her. The tranq slammed into her and she let out a cry of fury. In the next second, she was on that fool. She yanked the gun from him and slammed it back against the side of his head. He went down.

Another tranq went into her back. Her lips parted and—

She fell. But Rose didn't hit the ground. Someone had caught her. She forced her eyes to stay open and she stared into a blue gaze…a gaze that held no emotion at all.

Gargoyle. "I told you…" His voice was still tinged with sadness. "You're going to die."

And her eyes closed.

***

Luke Thorne was the Lord of the Dark. He was the devil in disguise. He was the baddest of the bad. And he was pretty sure all of that shit should be on a t-shirt.

He flew back to his island, expecting to find his guards waiting to meet him on the dock. Guards. Friends—same fucking thing to him.

Only he didn't see Julian.

He didn't see Rayce.

He didn't even see Marcos.

And his boat was gone, too. *What in the hell?* Everyone knew the rule about his boat. *No one takes my boat.*

He stalked up to his house, royally pissed. It was a good thing he'd left Mina in their little slice of paradise. He was trying not to show his dark side to her, at least not too much. And the ass-kicking he was about to give? She wouldn't like it…because the woman had some kind of soft spot for Julian and Rayce.

Who had a soft spot for an assassin?

The same woman who loved the Lord of the Dark.

He used a burst of magic to make his front door fly open. "Hey, bastards!" Luke thundered but he *knew* they weren't inside. His senses were more acute than any shifters…

They weren't there, but his twin brother's stench was all over the place. Luke jerked to a stop. "Oh, hell, no." Leo had *dared* step foot on his island? Did he want a slow death? Was he begging for one?

But…Leo wasn't the only person he smelled there.

Rose had been here.

And…Leo started rushing through his house. He headed for the cells—cells he'd used to house some of the worst paranormal beings on earth. Those cells should have been empty.

One wasn't. A human was inside. A young kid who actually waved to him when Luke appeared.

"Uh, hi, there," the kid said. "I'm Francis, but my friends call me Frankie."

Did he look like the kid's friend?

Francis smiled. "Is it time for me to go home yet?"

"What in the fuck is happening?"

CHAPTER SIXTEEN

Julian had to ditch his motorcycle. The swamp was too thick and he knew he could travel a whole lot faster on foot…and in panther form. So Julian jumped off the bike and yanked off his clothes. Then he was slamming onto the ground, hitting down on all fours as the beast clawed for his freedom.

And Rayce was right with him. When Julian's head swung to the right, he saw his friend shifting next to him. He didn't know where Leo was. They'd left the guy as a soggy heap back at the dock.

The panther bounded forward, flying through the marsh as he focused on Rose's scent. The dank earth was cloying, the swamp rotting, but she was sweetness in that hell. He was bound to her, and he followed her scent wildly. Desperately.

The wolf kept perfect time with him. They'd often run together in the past. Run together, hunted together, killed together, and he knew that before this day was done, they'd spill more blood.

Simon wasn't going to walk away. There would be no lenience from him. Julian intended to slice the man into pieces — him, and any of the goons who thought they could hurt the paranormals.

They ran and ran, and soon, the tall grass gave way to a clearing. But the panther and the wolf didn't burst into that clearing. Instead, they kept bodies low to the ground, using the tall grass as cover as they stared at the scene before them.

Two guards were at the door. Just two? *Insulting.* They'd take those bastards with no sweat. The building was long, stretching, with very few windows that he could see. A helicopter waited just a few yards away.

His nose twitched as a new smell reached him. *Brimstone. Magic.*

Trouble.

The same scent he'd caught on the boat, right before the freaking gargoyle had taken Rose away. His head turned, following that scent. A man stood there, right on the side of the building, using it for cover. The man's eyes were locked on Julian.

Julian bared his teeth.

The battle was on.

***

Rose woke to find herself strapped to a table. The straps were heavy and hard, cutting into her. She tried to break free, using her vamp strength but—

"You aren't going to get out," a woman's voice whispered. "None of us are."

Rose's head swung to the left. She could move her head, but her arms and legs and her torso were secured too tightly. She saw a cell— and a woman inside that cell. A woman with long red hair and tear-filled eyes.

"You're the last one," the woman said, her lips curving downward. "Now he's going to kill us all." She shuffled forward and her hands rose to curve around the bars. When she moved, Rose saw the big, black wings that sprang from her back.

"You're the angel." Her voice came out like a croak. Her body felt weak, her head foggy— stupid drug. "I know...someone who's been looking for you."

A mocking laugh came from the right.

Rose's head jerked toward that sound.

A blonde stepped forward. Her eyes were so dark they appeared nearly black. "No one's going to find us. He makes sure of that. Anyone lucky enough to get close...Simon just says they die, and they do. The dead are thrown to the gators.

The bodies picked clean. No one saves us. No one frees us."

"I'm…here to save us."

The blonde laughed again. "Sweetie, you're about to lose your heart. Those bands around you are made of metal that is a hundred times stronger than steel. And a drugged vamp? You're not going to break them. He's just going to break you. He'll break us all. Put the pieces together and then have what he wants most as he makes his own monster."

Her gaze darted around the room. There were two others cells there, but she couldn't see the people in them. It looked as if she was in some kind of lab. There was a surgical tray nearby. And lots of machines.

"Why is he collecting us?" Rose whispered.

"He's not collecting *us*. He's Frankenstein, and he just needs our parts." The blonde's voice was husky. Tired. How long had she been there? "He's ready to build now."

The door to that hellish place opened with a swish of sound. Simon strode inside. When he saw that she was awake, he hesitated for just a moment. "I'd hoped the drugs would keep you out longer."

She tried to fight back the weakness of her body. "Your…mistake."

"It is…but…I was trying to be kind. If you were out cold, you wouldn't feel the pain." He shrugged. "Oh, well. Guess this is really going to hurt you."

"*You don't have to do this!*" It was another woman's voice calling out. "There are other ways."

Rose glanced toward the cell near the blonde. A woman stepped forward, her skin a warm cream, her brown eyes filled with a terrible combination of sadness and terror. "Death isn't the answer."

"No, witch, you're right. It isn't the answer. Life is. And that's what you're all going to do. You're going to give me back the life that was taken away." He smiled. "Taken away by fucking monsters. You're going to give me back what I need, and she'll be stronger than ever. She'll never know weakness. She'll never know pain. She'll live forever."

Rose strained against the metal bands.

Simon picked up a knife. "I have everything I need. I just have to put the pieces all together…then my work will be done."

"Your…work?" she managed to croak.

He lifted the knife over her chest and then he sliced down, cutting right through her shirt. Right through the bra. He didn't cut her skin, though, not yet.

"The pieces I needed," he murmured. "The wings of an angel…"

"*You're the devil!*" The angel choked out.

He smiled. The tip of the knife pressed to Rose's chest, drawing blood. *"The eyes of a muse…"*

"You think I'm just going to let you *cut out my eyes?*" The blonde yelled. "You are such a freak! The power isn't even in my eyes — that's a legend! That's bullshit!"

The knife cut deeper. Rose didn't make a sound.

"The lips of a witch…"

"I say the spells, dumbass!" The yell seemed to echo around them. "It's not like my mouth is magic!"

The knife sank — hilt deep — into Rose's chest. "And the heart of the undead."

"You're…crazy," she gasped out. And she realized why she hadn't seen anyone in the last cell — that cell was for her. "This is just…nonsense. You aren't making…"

"I know magic." He smiled once more. She hated his smile. "I've made it my point to know ever since she was taken from me. Killed by a fucking beast. Her beautiful face slashed, her body torn."

He had a *knife* in her chest and he was talking about someone else being a beast?

"Okay, witch," the blonde muttered. Was she the muse? "You've got your fourth in here. Do your shit."

Rose had no idea what the muse was rambling about but...

The witch started chanting.

"Bend to break, bend to break," the witch called out. *"Bend to break, my fucking magic to take...bend to break..."*

Rose twisted her hands against the bands. Was it her imagination or did the band around her right wrist feel looser? Was it...bending?

"Bend to break, bend to break." Now the angel's voice was joining hers. *"Bend to break, my magic to take..."*

Simon ignored them. His eyes burned down at her. "You think humans are helpless? I learned the magic to change life. To imprison. To control. I learned the darkest powers when I first began to hunt. I learned that with the right pain, any creature can break. And that was my key. I broke so many, but I found my way back to her."

He started...moving the knife. Cutting her chest.

He's cutting out my heart. Rose screamed.

"Bend to break," the blonde's voice — the muse — was the loudest of all. *"Bend to break, my magic to take. Bend to break —"*

"You're extra special, you see," he kept cutting, still ignoring the other women as if they were of no consequence. "Because you weren't born to be a vampire. You were a human who was made — you're the one with the magic of rejuvenation that I need. You came back from death once. You were brought back. And your heart will bring her back, too."

"Who?" God, she *hurt!* "Who are you bringing back?"

He paused. "My Helene. My wife. A beast took her, but I will make her live again. She *will* come back to me. I'll pay any price. I'll do anything…" The knife cut again. "Just like your shifter."

No, no, he was *nothing* like Julian. Not a damn thing. And he was cutting her heart out of her chest while she just lay there, trapped.

"You know why you were warned never to be staked or burned?" Simon asked.

Her chest felt as if it were on fire.

"It's because Luke Thorne wanted to protect your heart. He knew it was the center of your magic. A heart that came back from death to beat again, a heart that was brought back not through the bite of a vampire, but through pure dark magic." He exhaled. "The perfect heart for me."

And he pressed down with the knife again.

"No!" The cry broke from Rose…and so did the band around her right wrist. Her hand flew up and locked around his hand.

He stilled. His eyes had gone wide with shock.

"My heart isn't…for you." Her breath heaved out. "It…already belongs…to someone else."

Then she twisted his wrist. He was leaning over her, shocked, and she used that against him. She drove the blade into his chest.

He lurched away from her, but it was too late. The knife was hilt deep in him. He staggered back then his knees seemed to give way as he fell to the floor.

Her breath heaved out. "Okay, okay...keep up that chanting...*and get me out of here.*" Blood pulsed from her chest. She was bleeding like a stuck pig, but she still had her heart. And Simon *wasn't* going to get it.

***

He heard her scream and the world fucking stopped for Julian. Rose's cry was full of pain and fear and he went a little crazy. He didn't shift back into the form of a man, he was too far gone for that. He leapt out of the grass and ran straight for the building.

He heard a wolf howl behind him.

The guards started screaming. They fired their weapons, but he dodged the bullets as they flew at him. The dirt kicked up near his body as the bullets thudded into the ground.

Then he was on the first guard. He slammed into the bastard and his teeth sank into the guard's throat. The man never had a chance to cry out.

"Freaking monster!" The other guard yelled. *"Go to hell!"*

Julian whirled around.

But the wolf beat him to the attack. Rayce jumped onto the other guard, sending him crashing down.

"Guess that means you have to deal with me."

Julian turned at the taunt. The scent of brimstone made his nose twitch. The guy was shifting in front of him, transforming into the stone figure of a gargoyle. Growing bigger, stronger, and standing between Julian and the thing that mattered most to him.

I'll get to Rose even if I have to claw this bastard apart.

Time to see if his panther's claws were really strong enough to cut stone. He was betting they were.

He growled then sprang forward. His mouth was open, his sharp teeth bared and —

The gargoyle was grabbed from behind. Hefted high up into the air by...Leo?

"My turn, you sonofabitch," Leo snarled. "Let's see how well *you* fly without your wings." Then he grabbed the stone wings and he shattered them in his grip. As the stone rained down, Leo shot higher and higher into the air, taking his captive with him.

One less problem.

Julian roared again and broke down the doors of that facility. An alarm began shrieking, loud enough to wake the dead, and more guards rushed toward him. They fired and he realized they weren't using tranqs when one of the bullets sank into his side. The bastards were shooting to kill.

He used his claws on the man to his right, raking him open. The other jerk who was trying to shoot him in the head? Julian tossed him through a wall.

Rayce rushed in behind him and the wolf leapt for the throat of a third guard.

Julian stood, his chest heaving, and he glanced around. His nostrils flared. He didn't hear Rose any longer but he could smell her...

Her blood.

Someone is about to fucking pay.

He raced down the hallway to his left. *I'm coming, love. I'm coming.* He'd promised to have her back, and he intended to always keep the promises he made to Rose. Always.

***

"Bend to break, my magic to take..." The witch was leading the chant. *"Bend to break, my magic to take..."*

The others were chanting with her, like a coven that had formed, and Rose could feel the power swirling in the air. *"Bend to break,"* she heard herself whisper. *"My magic to take…"* She thought the chant might be working. She could feel—

Simon lurched upright.

Oh, shit.

"He's still alive!" Rose screamed.

"No…" The muse had stopped chanting. Her hands fisted around the bars of her cell. "That's the problem. He hasn't been alive, not really, in a very long time."

Simon stared down at the knife in his chest. Then he looked up at Rose. "You bitch."

"You bastard!"

He grabbed the knife and pulled it from his chest.

She'd stabbed him in the heart. She *knew* she had. But…he was rising to his feet. He was walking toward her. His shirt was drenched with his own blood but he was *walking.*

He brought that bloody knife to her cheek. "Got a secret to share with you."

She didn't want to hear any of his secrets.

Her left wrist was almost free. The metal had bent, and if she could just slide her hand free…

"I don't have a heart. I cut it out myself, a long time ago. Because it hurt too fucking much to keep living without her and feeling so damn much."

Her gaze dropped to his chest. And…

Oh, sweet hell. How was that even possible?

Simon smiled at her. "But, unlike me, you won't keep going once your heart is gone."

"*Bend to break,*" the witch chanted. "My magic to—"

"*Shut the fuck up!*" Simon bellowed. Then he spun away from Rose and rushed toward the witch. "You think I'll stop with you? I'll go after your coven. Every single one. I'll burn those witches to ash. Say one more word. Utter one more chant, and I'll send my stone beast after them tonight."

She stopped chanting.

"Should have fucking thought..." Simon tapped the blade against his forehead. "I locked her magic down so it couldn't leave the cell, but you get enough creatures of power together...and you made a new circle, didn't you? A circle with just enough juice to bend those metal straps that hold my vampire." He laughed. "Clever, but the fun's over. Utter another word and everyone you all care about—" His voice boomed. "Will suffer! I will give them such agony you can't even dream about the hell they will face." He laughed. "Your precious husband, witch? I will make him scream. He will bleed and scream and the pain will *not* end."

The witch backed away from the bars of her cell.

"That's fucking right." He whirled from her cell and rushed toward the angel — the angel who retreated with a sharp cry.

Rose jerked against the straps. The metal didn't feel as strong and she was sure she could break free, if she just tried hard enough.

"Got to have more…" Simon was snarling. "Because of the vamp…she made me weak…"

She'd wanted more than him weak. She'd wanted him dead.

He put his index finger to the keypad near the angel's cell, scanning it, then he typed in a quick code. The cell sprang open.

"Leave her alone!" It was the muse who'd yelled. "You've hurt her enough! Just leave her *alone!*"

But he yanked the angel out of the cell. She fell to her knees and he lifted his knife. Her wings flew out, covering her.

And he stabbed them. Again and again.

"*No!*" The muse screamed. "Stop it!"

Every time that a feather fell from the angel's body, a flare of bright light shot toward Simon, as if power were running straight to him. His chest stopped bleeding. The wound sealed up.

He kept stabbing the angel's wings.

"*Stop it!*" Now the witch was screaming, too. "You're killing her!"

Simon laughed. "That's the point, isn't it?" But he took a step back. The angel lay huddled on the floor. "I need all the power from her wings if I'm going to get my Helene back. An angel's wings for magic. A muse's eyes for inspiration. A witch's lips for spells. And the undead's heart for life."

The strap on her left wrist snapped free.

Rose immediately grabbed for the metal straps that held her torso down. She would get free and he would *die*.

"No one can stop me now." He laughed and in a blink, he was at Rose's side again. He grabbed her hands and jerked them over her head. Then he pinned her wrists there, holding her easily with just one hand. His strength was incredible. Terrifying.

And he'd gotten it from an angel's wings?

How many feathers had he cut from the angel?

Simon leaned toward her. "Humans don't have to stay weak. We can take your power."

The wings...the feathers...that was how he'd been able to use a compulsion, one that hadn't broken without her blood to dilute his power. And now he was super strong, amped up on the magic of those wings like an athlete on steroids.

"I'll take that heart of yours," he said. "Right now." Only he wasn't using his knife. He drove his right hand straight into her chest.

Rose screamed in agony as she felt his fingers against her heart.

The door crashed in. A panther roared.

"What the hell?" Simon yelled as he let her go and whirled to face the new threat. "Why didn't my guards kill your ass? I *know* that was what I told them to do. Why is it so hard to find good help?" Her blood was on his fingers.

The panther roared again and leapt at him.

But when the beast hit him, Simon didn't go down. He caught the panther, holding him tightly, and laughed once more. "Surprise!" Simon tossed the panther across the room, and the great cat's body slammed into the wall, leaving a deep impression. "Guess who isn't going to lose this battle?"

The panther jumped back to his feet just as a big, white wolf burst into the room.

"Two of you?" Simon taunted. "How is that fair?"

The panther and wolf both launched at him. They all went down, crashing onto the floor as fangs and claws flew out.

Rose heaved against the bands. She broke two of them and slid her body out of the others, hauling herself up to freedom. She jumped off the table just as Simon heaved the wolf off him.

But he didn't escape from Julian. The panther locked his powerful jaws around Simon's neck. He bent down and she knew—

Simon's body jerked and went still.

She knew Julian had just severed the top of Simon's spinal cord, the way he'd told her that his kind attacked. But after that terrible bite, the panther didn't let Simon go. His head turned and his powerful teeth raked open Simon's throat, sending a spray of blood into the air.

"*Please, please say the panther is with you.*" The witch called out. "I *need* you to say that right now, vamp."

She took a step forward and pain burned through her chest. "He's…with me. So is the wolf."

And the wolf was rising right then. Stalking toward Simon and the panther but…

The panther swung his head toward Rose. She tried to smile at him, but it was hard considering she'd just nearly had her heart ripped out and Julian was covered in a dead man's blood.

The muse yelled, "We need to *hurry* here! Get us out, now! We don't have long before he's back!"

Back? *No, not again.* No way. The guy's head was barely attached to his body.

The panther's bones began to pop and snap. The wolf was already shifting, too.

"*Get us out!*" The muse jerked against her bars. "Hurry!"

Julian rose to his feet, once more in the form of a man. Rose ran to him, ignoring the blood on her, on him, and she threw herself against him. She held him tight, her body shuddering.

"I never, *ever* liked your plan," he rasped.

She hugged him harder. "We found them." She wouldn't explain just how close she'd come to losing her heart, not right then.

"How the hell do I get the cells open?" Rayce's voice blasted.

"You need his index finger...get the index finger from Simon's right hand," the witch yelled back. "And the code is 1031. Halloween...because the dick thought that was some kind of awesome joke. *But hurry, before he rises.*"

Julian stiffened. "Rises?"

Rose and Julian both whirled to look at Simon. He hadn't moved. His body was still splayed on the blood covered floor and his head was — yes, um, barely there. He didn't look like he was rising.

"He doesn't have a heart," Rose whispered. "He cut it out. I don't...how did he even live without a heart?"

But Julian swore. "Fuck. Sounds like he made a deal with someone..."

A deal?

And then understanding dawned. Of course, *of course.* A human *must* have made a deal to keep living that way. Humans couldn't work that kind of magic, not on their own.

But Luke Thorne would never make a deal with humans.

So that meant… "Where's Leo?" Rose asked, her voice sharp.

The ceiling fell in on them. Just gave way as something — someone — came crashing through it. Julian grabbed Rose, yanking her out of the way of the falling debris and shielding her with his body. And Rayce — he covered the angel who was still on the floor.

Dust and wood, metal and stone — they kept tumbling down.

"Where's the angel?" Leo's bellow. Because it had been Leo who'd come crashing through that ceiling.

And if anyone had made a deal with Simon Lorne, Rose knew it must have been Leo.

CHAPTER SEVENTEEN

Julian straightened. He and Rose turned to face the so-called Lord of the Light.

"This crap is why I said *hurry!*" The muse yanked against her bars. "Because trouble just keeps coming."

Leo glanced around, not appearing even a little concerned that two women were still caged—and that a seemingly dead man was on the floor, with most of his neck gone.

Rayce rose. The angel looked at up at him. Tears were on her cheeks.

"Dammit, why are shifters *always* naked?" Leo waved his hand and jeans appeared on both Julian and Rayce.

Julian growled. "You bastard. You did this."

Leo marched toward Rayce and the angel. "Gave you clothes? Yes, I did, you're welcome."

But Julian ran forward and grabbed Leo's arm. He swung the guy to face him. "*You* made a deal with Simon. Didn't you? You gave him some kind of power?"

"Get your hand off me. Panther, you don't want to piss me off."

"He had Rose on his table! Her blood was on his hands! You came to me, saying that some being called the Collector was after her. You said I had to protect her. You said I had to find him and stop him...so you could get your angel back." Fury shook each word.

Rayce moved closer to the angel. She hadn't spoken. Her head was down. She seemed to be staring at the feathers on the floor around her.

"You said you couldn't see the Collector's location." Julian's voice thundered out. "That he was using magic to block you."

"Maybe the witch was helping him," Leo said flatly as he inclined his head toward the cells and the witch who watched the scene with wide eyes. "Now, last warning, let go of me."

Julian didn't let him go. "I think Simon may have been getting a lot of help—"

The witch immediately denied, "It wasn't from me!" Then she shouted, "Assholes, will someone open the cell? *He will come back. He got too much power from her wings.*"

They needed to get out of those cells. Rose bounded to the body. She grabbed the fallen knife—the same knife that Simon had shoved into her chest—and she cut off his index finger. Then she ran to the witch's cell. She used the finger and she typed in the code. The door opened with a click.

"Thank you," the witch whispered. "I owe you."

"Get out of here," Rose said back. "You don't owe me a damn thing. Get to your family. *Go.*"

The witch looked over at Simon's body. "Fire."

Fire?

"Burn that bastard to dust."

Then she was rushing past Rose and heading through the open doorway.

"Uh, hello!" The muse's voice rang out. "Don't forget about me! Right here...a helpless muse. Not a bad girl, not really, just someone who *wants the hell out!*"

Rose hurried toward her cell. She used the finger and typed in the code as fast as she could. When the cell sprang open, the muse grabbed her and held tight. "I adore you. We are officially best friends forever." The muse squeezed her hard enough to take the breath from Rose. "But now I'm gone. And you'll never see me again." She turned and ran away.

Rose dropped the finger. She backed away from the cells. Her gaze flew to Julian and Leo — they were still glaring at each other with a dark and twisted fury.

"You helped Simon, didn't you?" Julian blasted. "You made some kind of deal with him.

Did you give him power? Why? Why the hell would you ever do that? Why—"

Leo drove his fist into Julian's jaw, but Julian didn't let him go. Julian's claws burst out and he raked them over Leo's chest. Blood soaked the Lord of the Light.

Julian's face had gone feral with rage. "*He was going to kill Rose! Why did you help him? Why did you lie to me? Why—*"

"You told him about the wings." The angel's voice was quiet, soft, and sad as it cut through Julian's roar. "I know that you did, Leo. You told him about the power in the wings. That the feathers can give life, can give strength, can give magic. Because there is no other form of pure power that can match an angel's wings."

Leo flinched. "Lila..."

"You made a deal with him." Her breath whispered out. "You gave him feathers, didn't you? My feathers. And he wanted more and more so he took *me*."

Leo broke free of Julian and lunged toward her, but Rayce stepped into his path, blocking him before he could touch the angel. "It wasn't like that."

"Then what was it *like*?" Julian demanded. "Explain it to me because I just don't get it."

Rose risked a fast glance at Simon. Was it her imagination or was that terrible wound in his neck closing? "Julian..." The witch had said fire.

And when she and Simon had gotten in that wreck, Simon had actually seemed panicked when he'd been trapped in the SUV. Because he'd feared burning? Flames *had* been erupting from the back of the vehicle.

Where the hell was fire when she needed it?

"His wife was murdered," Leo said. "Killed by a shifter—sliced apart while Simon watched. He wanted justice. He begged for it every night and so I thought...I might give it to him."

Rose rocked back on her heels.

"You made him your assassin," Rayce said. His gaze darted to Julian, then away.

But Leo had turned to fully face Julian. "Not so different from my brother after all, am I? I got tired of waiting for Luke to deliver justice. I had a human who wanted vengeance—vengeance he deserved. So, yes, maybe I gave him a few feathers. You don't send a lamb out to slaughter wolves without giving the lamb some weapons."

"He wasn't a lamb," the angel whispered. "And you aren't God. You don't get to decide who lives and dies."

Leo's face hardened. "He went after monsters—killers who tortured, raped and abused. He put them down but...problems arose. He wanted a new deal." He laughed. "I'm like Luke, and you Julian...you're just like Simon."

"No, he isn't," Rose snapped.

"Simon wanted his beloved Helene back. He would do *anything* to get her. Just like you, Julian. Weren't you ready to do *anything* to get Rose back?"

Julian's gaze jerked to her.

"Love," Leo spat. "It can make everyone weak."

Rose grabbed Julian's hand. "Or it can make you stronger."

But Leo shook his head. "I didn't agree to that particular deal, but Simon had learned too much already. He thought he could bring Helene back on his own…I told him it would be impossible to get the things he needed for a spell of that magnitude — "

"But he got them," the angel said, her voice a bit stronger. "He got *me*. I understand it all now."

Leo stiffened. "I came for you. I *found* you, Lila. You can go back to your old life now." He reached for her. "We're leaving this place, and you'll forget everything soon."

"I'm not going anywhere with you." She backed closer to Rayce.

Rayce growled. "You heard the lady."

"No!" Leo shouted. "That isn't part of the deal. The angel comes with me!" He glared at Rayce, then at Julian. "Panther, you want the deal we made finished, then you tell your wolf to back off. You want your *happy ending* — you give the angel to me now. If you make me fight you both, the deal is fucking *off.*"

The angel — Lila — grabbed Rayce's arm. "I can't go back. I feel too much…it will…it will break me. *I can't go back to nothing.*" Her body shuddered. "Please, don't send me back."

Rayce's face softened as he stared down at her.

"Wolf, you do not want to get in my way," Leo warned. "This fight isn't yours."

Rayce's head snapped up. He bared his teeth. "It is now."

Rose's gaze flew back to Simon. Her breath whooshed out. "He's coming back!" While they were dicking around and talking, the guy was regenerating right in front of them. "Where the hell can we get fire?"

"Fire?" Julian repeated. "I'll just take his fucking head. I won't leave a damn tendon connecting him this time."

And he leapt on Simon.

His claws flashed.

Simon's body jerked once more. His head rolled.

Julian looked up, chest heaving. "Easy enough." Blood dripped from his fingers.

Leo sidled next to Rose. "See what he is? Not even in panther form, but he's still a beast. A monster."

She bared her fangs. "So am I! Now get the hell out of here before you see just how evil *I* can be!"

Leo stiffened. "I was going to give your life back to you. That was the deal he made. The angel for you. I can make you human again. I can make you—"

"Keep your deal. I don't want to be human. I want to be exactly what I am…" She straightened her shoulders and stood to her full height. "I'm the vampire in love with a beast. And you…you can go screw off."

He blinked. "What? You—"

Rose heard the rush of the wind. She looked up and saw the dark shadow of wings…right before Luke Thorne flew through the hole that Leo had left in the ceiling.

Luke landed right beside his twin. His gaze raked the scene, taking in everyone and everything, including the body that was missing a head. "Did someone have a party…" he murmured, his sly smile flashing, "and forget to invite me?"

"Get Leo out of here," Rose snapped at him. "He's been helping that human over there—the one minus the head—your brother has been helping him take paranormals!"

"No," Leo denied. "I never *helped* Simon take them! He took them against my wishes—he stopped following my orders because he wanted his wife back! Why can't anyone ever just let go? Why can't—"

"Love." Luke had locked his hand over Leo's shoulder. "That's the shit you don't get. You think you're on the right side. Full of justice and might, but you don't understand anything. And there's about to be hell to pay for that crime." His powerful wings stretched behind him. He was going to fly away, to take Leo—

And hopefully drop him in an ocean or volcano or someplace where they wouldn't ever see him again. Only...

"Wait!" Rose yelled.

She felt Julian stiffen beside her. "You changed your mind," he muttered and there was pain in his voice. "You...want the deal?"

Changed her... "Never," she promised him. Her gaze met his, held. *"Never."*

The pain slid from his face.

"Uh, yes, I'm waiting, vamp," Luke pointed out.

Her head whipped back toward him. "I need fire." He could give her fire. "To kill Simon..." She pointed to the body. "I have to use fire."

Luke's brows climbed. "He looks pretty dead to me."

"He isn't!" Her breath heaved out. "He's been using angel wings to gain supernatural power. He's going to come back. I need to burn him—"

"To ash," Luke nodded. "Yes, you do…especially if he's been powering up on angel wings." He cast a pitying glance toward the angel. "Guessing my brother screwed you over, huh? Maybe Team Dark isn't looking so bad right now."

"Luke…" Julian growled.

He pointed at Rose. "Grab a board."

She bent down and picked up one of the boards that had broken down from the ceiling.

Luke snapped the fingers on his left hand.

Fire ignited on the end of her board, turning it into a torch.

"I could have just lit him up," Luke said as his gaze met hers. "But there are some things you like to do yourself, am I right?"

Yes, there were.

Her chest seemed to ache — her heart seemed to burn — as she walked toward Simon. She touched the torch to his shirt. His pants. The fire flared.

He burned.

The wind whipped as Luke flew up into the air, taking Leo away with him. And the whipping wind made the fire burn even faster, as if Luke had intentionally meant to stoke the flames.

Maybe he had.

Rayce picked the angel up into his arms and carried her out.

Rose stood right there, not moving until she was sure that Simon was gone. She wasn't going to look over her shoulder, always worried that he would reappear.

He was one monster that she *would* end.

When he was ash, she finally turned away from him. The torch still blazed in her hand even though the flames should have gone out long ago. Probably another bit of magic from Luke. When it came to fire, Luke always had total control.

Still holding that torch, Rose made her way outside. Julian followed right behind her, not saying a word. When she stepped outside, she realized the day had turned to night. Stars glittered overhead. They were so bright in the darkness.

She didn't see Rayce or the angel. And there was no sign of the witch or the muse. Everyone had vanished. She didn't blame them. She wanted to get away from that scene and forget the nightmare in the Everglades, too.

"You could've...had your life back."

"I like the life I have."

"You *hate* drinking blood."

"Not your blood." She loved the connection she felt when she bit him.

His face was tormented in the torch light. "You never wanted this. You never wanted—"

"I wanted you." There would be no more hiding. Not from him and not from herself. "I wanted you from the first moment I saw you, and yes, after my change, I was scared…but I still wanted you. I used to dream about you at night. I ached for you." She swallowed. "And I loved you." No, not *loved*. "I love you. I love you, Julian."

He didn't move. Why wasn't he moving?

"Ah, right, excuse me," Luke suddenly said as he stepped from the shadows. The guy had come back far faster than she'd expected. Luckily, Luke appeared to have returned alone. She didn't see Leo.

The torch jerked in her hand.

"I hate to interrupt sentimental moments, but we need to seal the deal."

Deal. She was coming to hate that word.

"Burn the building down, Rose. I'll make sure the fire doesn't spread from the scene. End this now."

She looked back at the building. And then she went forward, touching the torch to different spots of wood. Flames flickered. They grew. They spread.

She turned back to see Luke standing right beside Julian.

"You know what he is?" Luke asked her carefully.

She did. "The man I love."

"An assassin. A paranormal killer." He paused. "That was what he became...for you. Because he wanted you to live so much." Luke exhaled. "Can you live with that? Because if you can't, then walk the hell away now. It will be kinder to him." He waved his hand, and her torch sputtered out. "The fire won't spread. What happens next, it's up to you." The he looked up into the sky. "I have a dumbass twin brother to finish dealing with."

He flew away.

She dropped the chunk of wood and moved toward Julian.

"Don't."

She frowned. The flames crackled behind her.

"You...shit...you don't see it, do you? Leo was right. That bastard was right about one thing—I am like Simon."

"No." She stepped toward him. "You're not."

"I made a deal. I killed, for you. Simon killed—he killed because he thought he'd get his wife back."

Rose grabbed his arms. "Did you hurt innocents? Did you torture to steal power?"

"I *killed*. That's what I am. I'm a killer in my core and you...you have *always* deserved better. I knew it the first time I saw you. Beautiful Rose, with sunlight on your hair and sand between your toes. You deserved a life I could never give you." He swallowed. "Then I took your life away."

"No, no, you fought to keep me! I can see that now—"

His laugh was bitter and oddly broken. "What you need to see is that I'm a bastard. One who is so twisted inside he can't get past his own desires. I knew you wouldn't want to be a vampire, but I couldn't let you go."

"Julian, let's just…let's get out of here, okay?" Because he was scaring her. She'd said she loved him—several times now—and he hadn't mentioned love even once to her. Granted, it had been one hell of a day, so she was trying to cut the guy a little slack, but the fear still coiled inside of her. "Look, there's a chopper right there. You're the tough, do-anything-type, so my money says you can fly that bird—"

"I can."

"Then get us out of here. Take us—take us some place where we can be alone. Where we can start over."

"There isn't any going back." Deep lines bracketed his mouth. "I learned that a long time ago."

"Julian…"

But he caught her hand and pulled her toward the chopper. He lifted her up and made sure she was buckled in her seat. He took the pilot's spot and pushed some buttons and soon they were lifting up into the air.

She looked down and saw the smoke drifting up to them. A line of blue light surrounded the outskirts of that burning building, and she knew she was staring down at Luke's magic — containment for the fire.

The blades whirred overhead as Julian flew them away.

***

Julian landed the helicopter on Key West, on a private helipad that Luke owned. Sometimes, he felt like his buddy owned half of the damn world.

Because he did.

The blades stopped spinning, and his head turned so that he could stare at Rose. Beautiful fucking Rose. The woman he wanted more than anything.

The woman who'd said she loved him.

The deal was supposed to save her. It didn't work out that way. I screwed things up. I have to make it right for her.

"Why...why do I feel like you're about to tell me good-bye?"

Because he was. "Twenty-four, seven protection, remember? But only until—"

"The threat is gone."

He nodded. "Considering you burned the Collector to ash, I don't think we have to worry about him any longer."

"I told you I loved you."

He flinched.

"Don't you love me?"

"I'm a fucking selfish bastard."

"Julian…"

"I saw you on the beach…you were picking up sea shells. I saw you, I wanted you, and I didn't care about the rules that said I was supposed to stay away from a human. I was arrogant and cocky. I thought I'd screw you and walk away and no one would know that I'd broken one of Luke's famous laws." His hands clenched. "Shifters are supposed to stay away from humans. We're too rough. Too wild. I've known shifters who've killed human lovers."

"You didn't hurt me and you sure *didn't* walk away."

"Because I couldn't. Once wasn't nearly enough. I had you, and I wanted more." He'd wanted forever. But forever had ended in a hail of gunfire.

"I wanted more, too," she whispered. Did the woman have any idea the damage she was doing to him? His heart was in pieces. She'd gutted him with her love.

"You didn't want to be a vampire, Rose. You wanted a husband. A home. Kids. Holidays and trips to Disney World. You didn't want me. How could you? You didn't even know me, not really."

She grabbed his hand, her fingers curling over his clenched fist. "I know you now. I know you as a beast. I know you as a man. And guess what? I *still* want you." Her breath heaved out. "But what do you want, Julian? How do you feel about me?"

I love you. Completely. And that was terrifying. "If you died tomorrow, what do you think I'd do?"

She blinked.

"If I'd gotten to that fucking pit in the Everglades five minutes later and that bastard had taken your heart...what do you think I would've done?"

"Julian—"

"*Anything.* I'd do *anything* to get you back." That was the part that tore him up. "You say I'm not like Simon. You're right. In some ways, I'm worse. Because I wouldn't have fucking dicked around like he did. I would have moved heaven and hell *immediately* to get you back. I would have traded any life to have you back. You think I wouldn't kill an innocent to get back the woman I love?"

"You love me?"

Always. "I would kill anyone. I would trade anything...I would do *everything* to get you back.

Because I am a monster in my soul. And monsters aren't supposed to love because when we do, we just destroy. The love we feel is selfish and addictive and it's not right for you."

She shook her head. "No, you don't get to say what's right."

"I *mated* you, and I didn't even tell you!"

Her eyes widened. "Wh-what?"

"When we made love, I bit you. I marked you." His hand slid from hers and touched her on the shoulder. That sweet curve that led up to her neck. His fingers trailed over her silken skin. "When you mark here, that's a mating bite for my kind. Fucking binding as marriage. I'm locked to you, tied to you now for the rest of my life. I won't ever be happy with anyone else." He'd never feel so much as a flicker of desire for anyone else. He couldn't. He was mated and that meant that he belonged — body and soul — to her.

"I don't really want you happy with anyone else," she muttered.

She didn't get it.

"If you were a shifter, the marking would have just condemned us both to a life where we were always tied to one another. If you left me, you'd mourn for me. Your body would *hurt* because you needed me close to you." He exhaled. "But you're not a shifter, thankfully. So the rules that apply to me...they won't apply to you. You can walk away. You can be happy without me. You can have a life that isn't tied to a monster."

"And what about you? Will you be happy without me?"

Never. "I will be happy…knowing that you're safe. Knowing that you have a life that suits you better."

"You're…you're telling me to walk away."

He was trying to get her to run away. "Being noble isn't something I do well." Or at all, usually. "I am the monster in the closet. The one that little kids are supposed to fear. I'm a nightmare, and I don't know how to handle anything good." His hand lingered against her skin. "When I try, I destroy it." Just like he'd destroyed her. "You need someone better than me. You need to go…you need to just…leave, Rose. Live your life."

"Without you." She shook her head. Tears gleamed in her beautiful eyes. "Why are you doing this?"

"Because, for once, I want to put someone else first. I don't want to be like Simon. I don't want to take and take and take…until there is nothing left of you."

A tear slid down her cheek. "But I thought…"

He forced a hard smile. "That we'd get a happy ending? That's not for people like me. The ending I wanted…I wanted a redo for you. I wanted Leo to make you human again, and then I was going to get him to make you forget me."

She sucked in a sharp breath. "What?"

"We weren't going to be together when this story ended. You were going to have your life, and I was just going to be a bad dream that faded away when you woke up at dawn."

"You were going to do that—to me?" And she jerked away from him. She fumbled with the door, and she shoved it open, sending a crack snaking along the glass with the force she used. "You bastard!"

She jumped out of the chopper. He didn't follow her.

"You don't get to decide my life! I've learned to be a vampire and you know why? Not because I'm evil or dark or any crap like that...but because I'm strong." Her hand gripped the door. "I'm strong enough to keep going even when I was so terrified of the world around me. I'm strong enough that I learned to hunt, learned to live a whole new life. If I didn't want this, I could have given up at any moment. You think Luke didn't offer me a way out?"

"*What?*" Shock froze his heart. No, no, Luke would not have done that. He'd known just how desperate Julian was for Rose, how much he cared for her. He would *not* have offered her death.

"When I opened my eyes, he immediately started telling me the ways that I could die. He was giving me an out right then."

Julian shook his head. No, Luke had just been warning her...hadn't he? Doubt gnawed at him as he started to see the past with different eyes.

"And he came to me later...when I was so afraid of killing someone else, and he had a wooden stake with him. He told me...he told me that I wouldn't even feel the pain, if that was what I wanted."

For an instant, the whole world went dark. Rose—dead? Luke had gone to her with a stake. *I will kill him.* "The *sonofabitch* never told me—"

"That he offered me death? He did, but I didn't want death. I wanted to keep living. I chose to keep going. It's been my choice all along. Just like you have been. I want you, Julian. I love you. Beast or man, it's the same to me. *You* are the same."

"Rose..."

"It's time for *you* to make a choice." She let go of the door and stepped back. "If you want me, then we're looking to the future. There is no more guilt and no more regret. No more fear, not for either of us."

She still didn't get it. "I will destroy you." As he'd destroyed others. He didn't get out of the chopper. If he got out, he'd touch her. If he touched her, he'd be lost. She'd be lost. *I'm mated to her. There will never be another for me. But she still has a chance.* Why couldn't she see that? "I'm good for one thing in this world." He looked down at his hands and saw the claws that had sprung forth. "Killing. It was what I was born to do. It's what I've spent *years* doing. That shouldn't touch you. That blood and death —"

Her husky laughter cut him off. "Oh, Julian...I'm a vampire, blood and death are my life. They are the only things I know."

Because of him.

His breath sighed out. "I stayed away from you...because I didn't want to hurt you. I need you too much. I want you too much. When other men are near you..." He looked over at her. "I want to rip them apart."

She stared back at him. "That's called jealousy. It's normal."

It was normal for a human. "My control is razor thin when it comes to you. Others might *want* to rip apart another male who comes too close, but I can actually do it. It wouldn't even take effort. One swipe of my claws, and death follows."

"You wouldn't do it."

That was where she was wrong. He just stared back at her, willing her to see him for who he truly was.

"Why can't you see?" Now her voice was sad. "You're looking in a broken mirror. That's not who you are."

It was exactly who he was. "You should step away from the helicopter."

A furrow appeared between her brows. "What?" Her eyes widened. "You're *leaving* me?"

He was setting her free. There was a difference.

"You bastard! I love you, and you're walking—flying—away from me?"

He didn't speak.

She did. "I never thought you were a coward." Her words were low, but he heard them clearly. "You're afraid, aren't you? So afraid of what *could* happen that you won't let us have a chance together."

It wasn't a matter of *could*. The past spoke for itself. The past—their past. Her death. Because of him. And the whole tangled shit with the Collector? It went back to him. Julian had gotten her turned into a vampire. If he hadn't done that, she never would have been on the Collector's radar. She never would have been living with monsters.

"You blame yourself for everything, don't you?"

"For all the pain you've felt..." And there had been so much since she'd ended her human life. "Yes," he rasped. "It's on me. It will *always* be on me. I can't undo it, but I can stop it from happening again. I can make sure that I don't cause you to suffer more. When you walk away from me, you'll be safe."

"And what will you be?"

Empty. Broken. Alone.

A killer. "What I was always meant to be."

Her hair began to blow, tossing back against her face. Her clothes pressed to her body. He hadn't yet made the helicopter blades spin, so that rush of wind wasn't coming from him. If it wasn't from him...*oh, bugger.* "Rose, get back in the chopper." He lunged for her.

"*Now* you want me back?" she demanded and retreated a step. "I've had a really shitty day, so you need to make up your mind, panther."

Leo landed at her side. "We had a deal." His face was flushed and twisted in anger. "And no one breaks my deals."

Rose spun toward him.

He locked her into his arms and shot into the sky.

"No!" Julian bellowed. No, that SOB wasn't supposed to take her away. He slapped at the controls and the blades began to spin, faster and faster. The chopper lifted into the air and he raced after Leo.

CHAPTER EIGHTEEN

Leo landed on a beach — a star-shrouded beach that was far too familiar to Rose. "Luke's island?" She jerked away from him and her shoes sank into the wet sand. The waves rolled onto the beach. "What, do you seriously have a death wish or something?"

"Maybe." He crossed his arms over his chest. "I also don't have much time. Your lover *would* have found a damn chopper to use so he'll be here soon. Another problem to deal with."

"You aren't hurting him!"

He sighed. "You don't want me to hurt him, he doesn't want you hurt…this love thing is so annoying."

Rose glared at him. "What do you want? Why did you take me?"

"He took you…because of me."

Rose spun at that soft, sad voice, and she saw the angel step from the shadows. Luke was right by her side. Actually, he was penning Lila to *his* side.

"Good," Leo snapped when he saw his twin. "At least someone knows how to hold up a deal." He motioned to Luke. "I get the angel, you get the vamp, and we're squared away."

Lila shuddered.

"She doesn't want to go back," Rose said, whirling to glare at Leo. "You heard her before! You can't *make* her go back."

"You don't understand what's happening here." He raked his hand through his hair. "Her mind...she's confused. Angels can't handle the load of emotions that humans — and other paranormals — have. She's feeling, for the first time ever, and Lila doesn't understand how dangerous that can be."

"I understand plenty," Lila responded. Her voice was lilting and warm. Exactly the voice that Rose imagined an angel would possess. "You're the one who doesn't get it. You think you can make things right, but it's too late."

"No." He shook his head. "I can't let it be. I can't fail you." He pointed to Luke. "Send her to me, and I'll send the vampire over — with the same gift I always promised Julian she would get."

Gift? "No," Rose said, then she shouted, "*No!* I don't want any gift from you. I don't want a human life. I don't want any kind of magical do-over. I want what I've got." In the distance, she heard the whir of an approaching helicopter. "I won't change."

"Rose…" Luke's voice drifted to her. "Are you sure? Do you know what you're giving up?"

She knew. She turned to face Luke. "Shifters aren't supposed to love humans. That's one of your precious rules, right?"

He gave a grim nod. "Shifters are too brutal, they can't—"

"They can love vampires, though. Can't they? Because a vampire can handle a beast."

Leo's hand curled around her shoulder. "You'd give up my gift for a shifter? You'd lose your life for him?"

He didn't understand. The angel was right. He was the confused one. "I'm not giving up anything. I'm choosing. And I'm choosing him." Julian had just better stop being a dumbass and choose *her* in return. She turned her head and stared at the angel. "So there's no trade here. Lila is free."

Luke exhaled. "I wish that were the case." He rolled back his shoulders. "But I hold no dominion over the light. *He* does." His eyes glowed in the dark. "I thought you still wanted to be human, Rose, so when Leo came to me, desperate because the angel had vanished with Rayce, I found them. I brought them back here."

A growl came from the darkness. Rayce's growl. "A *shitty* move," Rayce called out.

Leo inched closer to the angel.

Rose heard the pop and crack of bones. Somewhere in those shadows, Rayce was transforming.

"I hold no dominion over her," Luke said again. "But he does...and since I've brought her here..."

"She'll be leaving with me." Leo rushed toward the angel with a burst of speed. His hand reached out to grab her, but a giant white wolf appeared in his path.

And that wolf snapped at Leo's hand.

Leo yelled and jerked back, narrowly avoiding those razor-sharp teeth.

The wolf stood guard in front of the angel.

"*Angel!*" Leo bellowed.

The whir of the helicopter blades was even louder. Rose felt the rush of air against her back. The chopper was landing.

"*Angel, come to me!*" Leo ordered.

Lila took a wrenching step forward, as if she were a puppet, being pulled on a string.

Luke said he had no dominion over her. Leo controls her. She has to do what he says.

The wolf whined and bumped against her, but the angel kept walking with those hard, lurching steps.

"You tricked me," Luke said to his brother, and his voice crackled with anger. "You knew that Rose didn't want to go back, didn't you? But

you couldn't find the angel. You had to get her
close enough to hear your voice so you could
control her. *You used me.*" His eyes didn't just
glow now. They blazed.

Leo opened his hand to Lila.

She shook her head, but her hand rose, as if
she'd take his. As soon as they touched, Rose
knew Leo would spirit the angel away.

It's not right. It's not what she wants.

The wolf howled as he shifted back into the
form of a man. "Let her go, you bastard!" Rayce
demanded and then he was flying across the
sand.

The wind pounded into Rose's back. She
glanced over her shoulder and saw Julian
bounding from the helicopter. "Rose!" Julian
screamed. "*No, you can't take her!*"

But Leo wasn't there to take her. He was
about to take the angel who shook as she reached
for his hand. The angel who wasn't being given
the choice she wanted.

Screw this.

Leo was worried about the threat coming
from Rayce, but Rose was the one standing
closest to him. And had he learned nothing from
their last little episode? She shoved the angel to
the ground and Rose was the one who grabbed
Leo's hand. She jerked his wrist forward and her
teeth sank into him. His blood pulsed into her
mouth, hot and powerful, just like before.

"No!" Julian bellowed. "Rose, please, *no!*"

It was too late. She'd attacked. Leo yanked back beneath her touch but she didn't let him go.

"*Angel, get out of here!*" Rayce yelled. "Fly away—now!"

Now...while Leo was distracted.

Now...while Leo was weak.

But...oddly...she was the one who felt weak.

Rose and Leo both fell to the ground, their knees hitting the sand. She still didn't let him go.

She heard the rush of wings. That would be the angel, flying to safety. Getting far enough away from Leo that he couldn't control her. And then she felt hands on her. Strong, warm hands that were tipped with claws. Those hands pulled her away from Leo. She blinked and found herself staring up at Julian. She tried to smile for him.

Fear had deepened the lines on his face. "Oh, love, what did you do?"

She'd...helped.

"You're dead," Leo rasped.

Julian lifted her into his arms. "Watch your fucking mouth, bastard." Julian's hold tightened on her.

Leo surged to his feet. His blood dripped into the sand. "*That vamp is dead!*" He lunged for her and Julian, but Luke blocked him.

The twins faced off.

"I think you're mistaken," Luke murmured, his voice as gentle as a breeze. "You see...Rose is a vampire. That means she's under *my* dominion. A creature of the dark. You have *no* say about what happens to her. And if you so much as twitch in her direction...we'll finally have that battle that has been prophesized for centuries."

The waves crashed onto the shore.

Fire began to burn inside of Rose's body. Just like before...just like when she'd had Leo's blood in her and it had started to burn her up, from the inside out. "J-Julian?" Now she was the one afraid.

He stared down at her, and his bright eyes were all she could see. Everything else was getting too dark.

"She wasn't supposed to have my blood!" Leo yelled. "It is *poison!* She barely survived once — it will hit her even harder this time. She's dying! I wasn't threatening her — I was telling you what's happening. She's dead — and there is nothing either of us can do for her now!"

Julian's hold tightened on her.

She wanted to smile for him.

She couldn't.

"Love...don't go," he whispered.

"I...choose..." She had to say this. He needed to always know. "*You.*"

***

Her fangs were gone.

"Why doesn't the vamp have fangs anymore?" Rayce muttered.

Because something was fucking *wrong*.

Julian lowered Rose onto his bed. She'd been drifting in and out of consciousness while he carried her to the house. He'd begged her to drink from him, pushing her mouth to his throat as he hauled ass to get her to a safe place but...

Her fangs hadn't come out.

"It's okay, love," he said, hating the fact that his voice came out so rough and ragged, as if everything was very much *not* okay. "I'll take care of you." He slashed open his wrist and forced her to take his blood. It had worked before. It would work again.

The blood dripped into her mouth. Julian massaged her throat, forcing her to swallow. But...

Her body seemed to be getting warmer to the touch. Too warm. As if she were feverish.

"Drink, Rose. Drink for me."

A hard hand closed around his shoulder. "She can't." Luke's voice. Sounding sad. Luke was never sad. He didn't have time for emotions.

Julian didn't look back at him. "This happened before. She bit your asshole of a brother once before, and I gave her my blood and everything was fine." Her cheeks were flushed.

Not just her cheeks. Her neck, her collarbone. Her arms.

"She's burning up, from the inside out." Again, Luke's voice was sad. "It won't matter how much blood you give her. My brother wasn't lying. His blood is poison to vamps. She…didn't really survive the first time."

What? That was bullshit, of *course* she'd survived.

"The first time she had his blood, the poison got in her body."

Julian kept his hand to her mouth. "And I gave her my blood. I diluted that tainted crap of his. She came back *fine*."

"The poison stayed in her body, but it was dormant, waiting for another exposure. That's how it works. One bite to begin, one bite to end."

What?

"Her heart is going to burn up. She'll burn in front of you. You should…step back. Let her go."

Dazed, Julian couldn't move at all.

"Fuck," Rayce swore from the corner of the room. "I'm so sorry, man."

No, this wasn't happening.

He stared down at Rose. Her hair was spread on the pillows behind her head. It just looked as if she were sleeping. And he remembered another time…

Rose had been lying in a bed, blood on her body. She'd been so still. But she hadn't been warm to the touch. She'd been ice cold and he'd known he was losing her.

So he'd turned to Luke Thorne, and he'd made a deal. *"Bring her back, Luke. Change her. She can't die."*

The memories swirled through his mind.

"She's already gone." Luke had stared at him with no expression on his hard face. *"Mourn the dead, and move on."*

He'd hit Luke then. Punched him. Clawed at him. And Luke had just taken the blows. *"I can't lose her! She's the first thing in my life that matters — don't take her! Don't let anyone take her!"* And he'd been lost — lost to a fury and pain that had sent him out of control. He'd destroyed that room. Slashing the walls. Breaking the furniture. Turning his claws on himself…

My fault. I did this to her. My fault. Mine…

Luke had grabbed his hands. Julian's claws had been buried in his own chest.

"Why are you doing this?" Luke asked him.

"Because I should die. She should live." Simple. So simple…And if she didn't live…then he was ready to die.

"You…love her? You fell in love with a human, knowing it was forbidden?"

One of Luke's laws. *"I fell in love with her…"* He stared unflinchingly at the most powerful dark paranormal being in the world. *"Because I couldn't stop myself. She owns me. Owns me. And I can't just let her die!"*

Luke stared back at him. *"Too late, my friend. She's gone."*

He'd grabbed Luke by the shirt-front, his claws tearing into him. *"Make me a deal. You make deals with everyone else. Give her life back. Help me."*

"I can't," Luke gritted in response. *"To bring someone back from the dead? That would deplete my power. My enemies would close in. I would be done. The dark would fall."*

"I will take care of your enemies."

Luke's gaze had hardened. *"Be careful what you say."*

Rose was still and cold on the bed. *"I will hunt your enemies down. You know I'm the best hunter out there. You keep her in this world —"*

"It's not keeping her here. It's bringing her back. And believe me, there would be a heavy price for that. Both for me...and for you."

"I don't care about the price. I care about her. Only her. And I'll do anything..."

Then the deal had been set. Rose had come back.

"I tried to do the right thing," Julian rasped. His hand slowly lowered from her mouth. His blood had dripped down her chin. Steam seemed to rise from her body. "I was sending her away, trying to make her leave because I knew I was bad for her. I hurt the ones close to me, and no one has ever been closer than her."

Rayce cleared his throat. "Buddy, um, I think we should walk out now. There are some memories that you don't want to have. And your lady burning? You don't want to carry that memory."

His head turned so that he was staring at the wolf. "Do you think I would ever let her die alone?"

Rayce's jaw hardened.

No, dying alone wouldn't happen.

He used his claws to cut his wrist even deeper. "I just have to give her more blood. It worked before. It will work again."

"No," Luke told him. "I'm so fucking sorry, but it won't. My brother was made to be my opposite. His blood can destroy dark paranormals just as mine…mine destroys the light. We've both always known we were poison."

Mine destroys the light.

In a flash, Julian jumped off the bed. He grabbed Luke and slashed his claws across the guy's forearm.

The whole room seemed to shake — actually, it did shake. Luke's fury blasted against him. "What the fuck are you doing?"

Trying to save her! "Give her your blood. If he's poison to her, then you could be the cure. *Give her your blood.*"

But Luke didn't move. "Do you have any idea what you're asking?"

"I'm asking for you to help the woman I love." *Because I'm breaking apart without her.*

"My blood...you don't know what it will do to her."

Julian looked back at the bed and his heart nearly stopped. "She's dying already. What could be worse?"

"She could come back...*wrong.*"

What?

"You think I haven't already considered giving her my blood?" Luke shook his head. "But I don't know what will happen if I do. My blood...Leo's blood...all in one person? That much power? Light and dark trapped together? She could wake up and want only death for *everyone* around her. Or she could wake up...and think that monsters like you and me — the dark ones — that we need to be eradicated. *She* could be the instrument of our destruction. The being who takes us out. *I don't know what she'll become.*"

"I know what she'll be." His shoulders straightened. "Because it's what she's *always* been, vampire or human. She's no killing machine. She's not evil. She's not twisted. She won't ever be. You give her the blood, and she'll just be stronger. When bad things come her way, she just keeps growing stronger."

Luke studied him with worried eyes. "And you think *that's* not dangerous?"

"She'll be on our side," he promised. *Help her!*

"How do you know that?"

And despite everything, Julian managed to smile. "She chose me." *She chose life.* "And I chose her. She'll come back strong and she'll come back *right*."

"If she doesn't, will you be the one to put her down?"

The question seemed to echo around him.

And he didn't speak.

"That's what I thought," Luke said softly. "You love her, you *can't* kill her, but if something goes wrong, I'm supposed to just let her roam around attacking people? You know I can't do that. And you're the one I send when the dark ones go rogue. If you can't handle her, then what will I do?"

Did Luke really think he was going to promise to kill Rose?

"She's your weakness. You think I don't understand?" Luke sighed. "I do. But I have to look out for more than just you. She could be too strong. She could be—"

"She's dying." And he couldn't just do *nothing.* "This is Rose. *Rose.* She's always been good. She never — not once — killed anyone when she was a vampire."

Luke's lips twitched. "She used to get so nervous before drinking that she'd nearly faint. A vampire, fainting at the thought of *taking* blood."

"She hates using compulsions," Julian continued, frantic. "Because Rose doesn't like to control anyone. She wants people to have a choice. *She* chose to live this time. She was fighting for the angel. Fuck, she helped an *angel*. Doesn't that prove she'll never go so dark that she loses touch and hurts everyone?"

Luke's gaze drifted to the bed. "The angel will owe her…"

"Right, yes, fine, the angel owes her. The angel can pay her back…*if you help Rose.*"

"The angel can kill her."

Julian stiffened. "What?"

"Angels are so much stronger than you realize. If your lady goes rogue, the angel can kill her. She can pay the debt back that way." He nodded. "Fine. Done deal."

No, nothing was done. The angel would *not* kill Rose. She'd have to rip him apart first.

Luke paced toward the bed. He put his hand over Rose's mouth.

"Uh, yes, so glad we worked all that out." Rayce crept forward and the floor groaned beneath his feet. "But how are you going to make her *drink*? She's nearly gone…"

"Don't forget, I hold dominion over the dark." Luke was his confident self once more. "And there's enough of her still in that bed to *hear* me. Rose...*Rose, drink my blood.*"

He dripped the blood into her mouth.

Julian wasn't so sure that she *could* hear him, so he rubbed her throat, trying desperately to make her swallow...and she did.

Luke gave her more blood. She took it, but her eyes didn't open. And her skin was still too hot. "She's not getting better!"

Luke gave her more. Julian smoothed her hair away from her forehead. "Keep giving her—"

Her eyelashes fluttered. "No...more."

Luke immediately drew back.

Her breath whispered out and her gaze swung toward Julian. "I'm...okay?"

No, she was still hell hot and shaking. She was still terrifying him. But he smiled at her. "Of course. You're better than ever." Then he looked back at Luke and Rayce. "You two, get the hell out."

Because if something happened, if something went *wrong* as Luke had suggested, Julian would be there for her. He wouldn't leave her again. They'd face what came together, and he would sure as hell never be dumb enough to try and make her leave him.

The others filed out. The door shut behind them.

"So...hot..." Rose whispered.

He scooped her into his arms and strode into the bathroom. He yanked on the cold water and sent it exploding down as he stepped into the shower, still cradling her in his arms.

Steam rose when it hit her skin.

Just like before.

"Drink, love, drink from me." His blood could dilute what she'd gotten from Leo, from Luke...his blood could link them.

Her fangs pressed to his neck. A tender bite. Her tongue slid over his skin. And she drank.

They stood like that, in the shower, the water pouring down on him, her fangs in his throat, his arms around her...for an endless time. He didn't move. He was just happy to have her there with him. *Alive.*

Rose.

And...

Her fangs slid away from his neck. She kissed his throat. "Don't worry. An angel isn't going to have to...put me down."

He blinked, then looked at her.

She smiled up at him. The steam didn't rise from her skin any longer. She wasn't flushed. She was perfect. "And you don't have to kill me either."

"I *never* would."

Her eyes were bright. "I'm not wrong. I don't want to kill and maim everyone."

She was okay. His Rose was staring at him with her sweet smile and with love in her eyes. He had to choke down the lump in his throat. "That's…that's good to know."

Her smile stretched. "I'm okay?" This time, it was a question.

"You're better than okay." He kissed her. Deep. Hard. Wild. His heart was about to burst out of his chest and he was just so —

Happy.

Yeah, that was what he fucking was. He was happy. Rose had always made him happy.

Her tongue slid against his lip. She kissed him back with the same passionate intensity and in the next moment, Julian was jerking off her jeans. He shoved her jeans to the bottom of the shower and ripped away her panties.

"Tell me to slow down," he begged because he knew he was going too fast. Too fast. Too rough. Too wild.

She laughed — the sweetest sound in the world — and her hands reached for the top of his jeans. "Don't you dare."

He stilled and stared into her eyes.

"I almost lost you. I almost lost us both," she whispered. "And you think I want to go *slow* now?" She rose onto her tip toes and nipped his bottom lip. "Not on your life, panther."

She still owns my heart. She always will.

She lowered the zipper of his jeans. He lifted her up against that shower wall. The water was ice cold, but he didn't care. He had his whole world in his arms.

He thrust into her. They both groaned. She was tight and wet and so perfect...

His.

He withdrew, then thrust deep. Again and again and he stroked her clit, wanting to push her to the edge before he came. He wanted her lost to the pleasure. To feel. To love.

She cried out his name. He felt her sex clench around him, and he pumped even harder into her.

Then he exploded within her. A long, hot release as his body shuddered.

Her arms were around him. She held him tight.

As tightly as he held her.

The cold water kept falling onto them. He forced his head to lift. He should move them. Get her dry. Get her warm.

But instead, he kissed her. He'd always loved her mouth.

And when he pulled back, she was smiling at him.

The most beautiful woman in the world...the woman who'd gone through hell and come back…was smiling at him and staring at him as if…

As if I'm not a monster.

"Tell me you love me," Rose whispered.

"I love you." He'd tell her that a thousand times. A million. Every day for the rest of their very long lives. Because maybe…when he'd first got Rose to come back as a vampire…maybe he'd made a secondary deal with Luke.

I wanted to always be around to protect her. To be there, whenever she needed me.

And Luke had given him that extended life…for a price.

There is always a price with him.

Luke's words whispered through his mind. *As long as you walk the earth, you'll swear to stand at my side. When the battle comes between me and Leo…you will stand with me.*

He'd already planned that particular stand, so agreeing hadn't been exactly hard for him.

"I'm not…wrong," she said. But then he saw fear flicker in her eyes. "Am I?"

He kissed her again. "No. You are the only right thing in my world." He believed that to the depths of his soul.

Her smile flashed again. The fear vanished.

"But, love, do me a favor, okay? Promise me…" He turned off the blast of cold water with a flip of his wrist. "Don't *ever* drink from Leo or Luke again."

"I promise."

He lifted her into his arms again. He loved to hold her. He just fucking loved her. Julian gazed into her eyes.

"Julian? Are you sure...I...is something wrong?"

"No, it's right." Finally. The guilt was gone. The fear was gone. For them both. They'd chosen...each of them. And they'd chosen life.

Love.

She curled her arms around his neck. "Take me to bed. I've really had one hell of a day."

Laughter came from him. Laughter...after everything. Only Rose could make him feel that way.

"If you think today was interesting...just wait until you see what our nights will be like." His lips pressed to hers. The kiss wasn't rough or wild. It was sweet. Tender.

"Promises, promises..." Her voice was a husky temptation.

But... "Yes." He nodded once. "I do have promises. I promise, I will love you forever. I promise...I will never let go."

Her breath sighed out. "I'll hold you to that."

And he'd hold her. Forever.

CHAPTER NINETEEN

Two weeks later…

"You know everything about me." Julian's voice was deep and dark and it made Rose want to shiver. They stood on the balcony, the ocean pounding against the beach below them, and she knew she was in heaven. "The good and the bad. The dark sins that stain my soul."

"I rather like your soul." Her hand reached up and curved along his jaw. The rough stubble slid over her palm. "Because I love you."

"You don't see a monster, do you?"

Rose shook her head. "I only see you."

"Maybe I should have stayed away from you…"

"You most *definitely* should not have." The pain, the fear — it had all been worth it. Wasn't love worth fighting for? Especially a love that was going to last forever.

"I saw you and I knew my world would change."

She had to look away from him for a moment. This talk…it was so much like the one they'd had—a lifetime ago. When a panther shifter had tried to convince a human that monsters were real.

And then death had come.

"I saw you, and I knew what I'd always been missing. For the first time, I felt complete."

That was sweet. Her gaze slid back to him. Her big, bad panther...and he was standing before her, exposing his soul.

"I *never* wanted you to fear me."

"I don't. I never will again." Trust went soul deep. She smiled at him. "I think you were made for me."

His eyes widened. Did he remember that he'd once told her that exact same thing? Julian cleared his throat. "And I was made for you."

He *did* remember. Because those words had been the ones she'd given to him, so long ago.

It was all the same except...

This night wasn't going to end with her dying. No bullets were flying at them. Stars glittered overhead and the scent of the ocean teased her nose and—

Julian had dropped to one knee.

She tried to fight her smile. She couldn't. Just like she couldn't make her heart stop racing.

"Rose, will you—"

"*Yes!*"

"Marry me?" Julian finished. Then he blinked. "Wait, yes?"

She grabbed him and yanked him back up—
the better to hug him and kiss him like mad.
"Yes, absolutely, yes!" Marriage. Forever. She
wanted it all.

They would have it all.

Who said monsters didn't get a happy
ending?

They did. They fought like hell for those
endings...they fought like hell for each other.

His arms closed around her, and she knew—
Rose *knew* that life was just beginning. Her life
with Julian. Her life without fear.

Her life...her choice.

And it was going to be amazing.

***

Julian was laughing.

Kissing his mate, laughing, and disappearing
as he led his vamp back into the house.

"Looks like someone's happy."

Luke sighed when he heard his brother's
sardonic voice. "No thanks to you." He turned to
face Leo, not in the mood for this shit. "We need
to clear the air."

"Is that why you summoned me?" Leo's
brows rose. "Because I thought you'd banished
me from this island—"

"After you tried to kidnap the angel and you nearly killed Rose?" His arms crossed over his chest. "Yes, you're not exactly welcome."

Leo glanced toward the house. Luke thought he saw a flicker of fear in his twin's gaze. Interesting. Did he fear the panther? Or the vampire?

"Is she...wrong?"

"No, I think she's quite right. Finally." Rose wasn't fighting who she was any longer. She'd embraced her vamp side. She'd let go of her fear. And she was loving — wildly, fully, without reservation. She was good and so was Julian.

Luke figured they deserved their happiness...and speaking of what people deserved. "I'm missing...one of mine."

Leo shrugged. "What does that have to do with me?"

"Simon Lorne was using a gargoyle to do his dirty work. The last time the gargoyle was spotted, well, Rayce told me that *you* picked him up and flew away with the guy."

"He was on Simon's side. He needed to be put down."

Luke didn't let his anger sweep out — it was too dangerous when he did. "If this is the gargoyle that I think it is...he was under a spell." He had been, for a very long time. "Where, exactly, did you *put* him down at?"

Leo glanced back toward the ocean. "Stone sinks pretty quickly. If I were you, I might try the deepest depths."

"You're such an asshole."

Leo smiled. "I could give you more of a map, if you were...say...willing to help me find a certain angel?"

Luke just stared at him.

"Do we have a deal?" Leo prompted.

"No."

A faint rustle of sound came from behind Leo. It was the only warning his brother got. Leo whirled — and found himself face to face with Julian.

"I wanted to give my friend a wedding present," Luke announced. "I figured he'd like a bit of payback."

Julian's claws slashed, cutting into Leo. Leo screamed and his wings shot from his back even as the blood poured from his chest. Then Leo was shooting up into the air —

But Julian's claws caught one wing. They ripped it apart. Leo fell like lead onto the ground.

Julian started to go after him again.

"That's enough." Rose's voice.

Luke smiled. "Sweet Rose, ever the voice of reason." He strode toward his brother, and, for fun, gave him a little kick in the side. "You're lucky she didn't come back wrong."

Leo groaned.

"Payback," Julian snarled. "It's a bitch."

Or a very, very enraged panther.

Rose twined her fingers with Julian's and they headed back toward the house.

For a moment, Luke just studied his brother. Then he smiled. "You're not healing as quickly as you once did."

Leo sat up, glaring.

"I think…you may be weaker, brother. A bite from a vampire can have repercussions, especially for someone like you." He laughed. "You were worried about her being wrong, but maybe you should worry about yourself. Claws would never do this much damage to you before."

Leo had gotten to his feet. He stumbled a bit, glaring. Scales began to appear on his body. He was transforming fully. The best way to heal from injuries.

Luke didn't speak again, not until his brother had flown away. For years…*years*…centuries…there had been talk of a battle between him and Leo. He'd worried about the day when that final fight would come. Good versus evil. Blah fucking blah.

He'd worried but now…

Now he laughed again.

Because his dear twin was showing a weakness, and if there was one thing Luke knew how to do…it was exploit a weakness.

He turned and strolled back to the house. But he didn't get far, not before a wolf shifter crossed his path.

"Glad you think the night is funny," Rayce muttered. "That bastard is probably off, hunting down that angel right now."

Luke clamped a hand over his shoulder. "Why not make this a challenge?"

Rayce lifted a brow.

"You have her scent. Why don't *you* see if you can find her first?"

The wolf gave him a slow smile.

And the game was on.

THE END

###

If you enjoyed ON THE PROWL, be sure to look for BROKEN ANGEL, Book 3 of the Bad Things series, in December of 2016.

A NOTE FROM THE AUTHOR

Thank you so much for taking the time to read ON THE PROWL. I hope that you enjoyed the story. I've been having such an amazing time writing about the "Bad Things" — and there are more stories coming soon! Next up, I'll be releasing Rayce and Lila's story in BROKEN ANGEL. And soon…I'll have a gargoyle hero to share with you.

If you'd like to stay updated on my releases and sales, please join my newsletter list www.cynthiaeden.com/newsletter/. You can also check out my Facebook page www.facebook.com/cynthiaedenfanpage. I love to post giveaways over at Facebook!

Again, thank you for reading ON THE PROWL.

Best,
Cynthia Eden

www.cynthiaeden.com

ABOUT THE AUTHOR

Award-winning author Cynthia Eden writes dark
tales of paranormal romance and romantic
suspense. She is a *New York Times, USA Today,
Digital Book World,* and *IndieReader* best-
seller. Cynthia is also a three-time finalist for the
RITA® award. Since she began writing full-time
in 2005, Cynthia has written over fifty novels and
novellas.

Cynthia is a southern girl who loves horror
movies, chocolate, and happy endings. More
information about Cynthia and her books may be
found at: http://www.cynthiaeden.com or on
her Facebook page at:
http://www.facebook.com/cynthiaedenfanpage.
Cynthia is also on Twitter at
http://www.twitter.com/cynthiaeden.

HER WORKS

Paranormal Romance

Bad Things
- The Devil In Disguise (Bad Things, Book 1)
- On The Prowl (Bad Things, Book 2)

Blood and Moonlight Series
- Bite The Dust (Blood and Moonlight, Book 1)
- Better Off Undead (Blood and Moonlight, Book 2)
- Bitter Blood (Blood and Moonlight, Book 3)

Purgatory Series
- The Wolf Within (Purgatory, Book 1)
- Marked By The Vampire (Purgatory, Book 2)
- Charming The Beast (Purgatory, Book 3)
- Deal with the Devil (Purgatory, Book 4)
- The Beasts Inside (Purgatory, Books 1-4)

Bound (Vampires/Werewolves) Series

- Bound By Blood (Bound Book 1)
- Bound In Darkness (Bound Book 2)
- Bound In Sin (Bound Book 3)
- Bound By The Night (Bound Book 4)
- Forever Bound (Bound Books 1-4)
- Bound in Death (Bound Book 5)

Night Watch Series
- Eternal Hunter (Night Watch Book 1)
- I'll Be Slaying You (Night Watch Book 2)
- Eternal Flame (Night Watch Book 3)

Phoenix Fire Series
- Burn For Me (Phoenix Fire, Book 1)
- Once Bitten, Twice Burned (Phoenix Fire, Book 2)
- Playing With Fire (Phoenix Fire, Book 3)

The Fallen Series
- Angel of Darkness (The Fallen Book 1)
- Angel Betrayed (The Fallen Book 2)
- Angel In Chains (The Fallen Book 3)
- Avenging Angel (The Fallen Book 4)

Midnight Trilogy
- Hotter After Midnight (Book One in the Midnight Trilogy)
- Midnight Sins (Book Two in the Midnight Trilogy)
- Midnight's Master (Book Three in the Midnight Trilogy)

Paranormal Anthologies
- A Vampire's Christmas Carol

Loved By Gods Series
- Bleed For Me

ImaJinn
- The Vampire's Kiss
- The Wizard's Spell

Other Paranormal
- Immortal Danger
- Never Cry Wolf
- A Bit of Bite
- Dark Nights, Dangerous Men

Romantic Suspense

Killer Instinct
- After The Dark (Killer Instinct, Book 1) - Available 03/28/2017

LOST Series
- Broken (LOST, Book 1)
- Twisted (LOST, Book 2)
- Shattered (LOST, Book 3)
- Torn (LOST, Book 4)
- Taken (LOST, Book 5) - Available 11/29/2016

Dark Obsession Series

- Watch Me (Dark Obsession, Book 1)
- Want Me (Dark Obsession, Book 2)
- Need Me (Dark Obsession, Book 3)
- Beware Of Me (Dark Obsession, Book 4)
- Only For Me (Dark Obsession, Books 1 to 4)

Mine Series
- Mine To Take (Mine, Book 1)
- Mine To Keep (Mine, Book 2)
- Mine To Hold (Mine, Book 3)
- Mine To Crave (Mine, Book 4)
- Mine To Have (Mine, Book 5)
- Mine To Protect (Mine, Book 6)

Montlake - For Me Series
- Die For Me (For Me, Book 1)
- Fear For Me (For Me, Book 2)
- Scream For Me (For Me, Book 3)

Harlequin Intrigue - The Battling McGuire Boys
- Confessions (Battling McGuire Boys...Book 1)
- Secrets (Battling McGuire Boys...Book 2)
- Suspicions (Battling McGuire Boys...Book 3)
- Reckonings (Battling McGuire Boys...Book 4)
- Deceptions (Battling McGuire Boys...Book 5)

- Allegiances (Battling McGuire Boys…Book 6)

Harlequin Intrigue - Shadow Agents Series
- Alpha One (Shadow Agents, Book 1)
- Guardian Ranger (Shadow Agents, Book 2)
- Sharpshooter (Shadow Agents, Book 3)
- Glitter And Gunfire (Shadow Agents, Book 4)
- Undercover Captor (Shadow Agents, Book 5)
- The Girl Next Door (Shadow Agents, Book 6)
- Evidence of Passion (Shadow Agents, Book 7)
- Way of the Shadows (Shadow Agents, Book 8)

Deadly Series
- Deadly Fear (Book One of the Deadly Series)
- Deadly Heat (Book Two of the Deadly Series)
- Deadly Lies (Book Three of the Deadly Series)

Contemporary Anthologies
- Wicked Firsts
- Sinful Seconds
- First Taste of Darkness

- Sinful Secrets

Other Romantic Suspense
- Until Death
- Femme Fatale

Young Adult Paranormal

Other Young Adult Paranormal
- The Better To Bite (A Young Adult Paranormal Romance)

Anthologies

Contemporary Anthologies
- "All I Want for Christmas" in The Naughty List
- Sinful Seconds
- All He Wants For Christmas

Paranormal Anthologies
- "New Year's Bites" in A Red Hot New Year
- "Wicked Ways" in When He Was Bad
- "Spellbound" in Everlasting Bad Boys
- "In the Dark" in Belong to the Night
- Howl For It

48268669R10173

Made in the USA
Middletown, DE
15 September 2017